The Picture Window

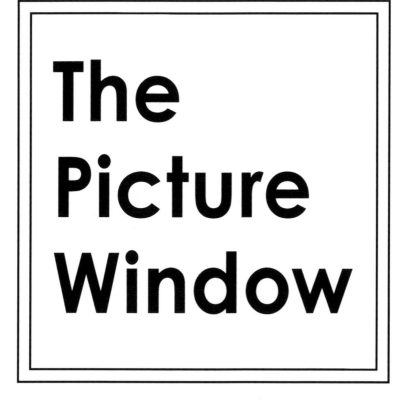

The Picture Window

CONNIE STOKES STOREY

WESTBOW°
P R E S S
A DIVISION OF THOMAS NELSON
& ZONDERVAN

WestBow Press books may be ordered through booksellers or by contacting:

WestBow Press
A Division of Thomas Nelson & Zondervan
1663 Liberty Drive
Bloomington, IN 47403
www.westbowpress.com
1 (866) 928-1240

ISBN: 978-1-4908-3440-5 (sc)

Library of Congress Control Number: 2014907171

Printed in the United States of America.

WestBow Press rev. date: 4/25/2014

Dedication

To my children, Neilie and Heather, and grandchildren: Jake, Jon, Ashlynn, Dalton, and Trey – so they may *know* what a special person their Grandmother and Great-Grandmother was.

Acknowledgment

To Georgia Clark Cason, Charles Fulghum, Eddie and Pearlene Yeomans Smith, Etta Mae Sowell, Betty Stokes, Jessi Bush, Chris Stokes, and Gwen Monroe for contributing facts and information valuable to *The Picture Window*.

And, last but not least, to my Father, Willie F. (Pete) Stokes, for time spent re-living the past and relating these events in numerous sessions with me. We cried and laughed together. Thanks, Daddy, for the memories!

Introduction

The Picture Window is based on the life of Quinelle Yeomans, a humble country girl from South Georgia.

The on-going scene is Quinelle reminiscing about her life while confined to a hospital bed placed in front of the picture window in her living room. Her body is ridden with cancer at the young age of forty-nine.

Her hopes, dreams, and life experiences are conveyed while holding on to her faith and belief that God will heal her.

A beautiful love story between Quinelle and her first love develops throughout *The Picture Window*. Their union is a perfect example of the wedding vow – "in sickness and in health".

My goal is that *The Picture Window* will be inspiring to help us all cling firmly to our faith, and have a life filled with hope.

The importance of family, church involvement, and faith in God made Quinelle the inspirational person she became. Quinelle had her share of struggles and heartaches. Some events told will make you cry; others will bring a smile to your face.

Delight in her life's journey as I put into words the joys and sorrows of a fine Christian woman determined to live her life as an example to others, and to win her battle with cancer.

The family, friends, and acquaintances in *The Picture Window* are real, and names have not been changed.

Prologue

Gazing out through the living room picture window, I can see the azaleas are in bloom. Spring is here once again. I can hear the birds chirping out their own individual songs. The dogwoods are ready to burst forth any day now with beautiful white blossoms. I can see that Pete will need to cut the grass around the ponds soon. He really enjoys getting on his tractor; whistling all the while, making our "paradise" here on earth as perfect and pleasing as he possibly can. Thus, the name of our little piece of heaven: "Pete's Paradise".

No longer able to climb the stairs to our bedroom, I am confined to this hospital bed parked in front of this picture window. This is all the world I see now.......getting so sleepy........ dogwoods seem to be blooming right before me.......looks a lot like cotton fields........hot and so tired......

Chapter 1

"Are we there yet?"

"Almost."

"It's so hot in this car! I can't breathe! Willene, what is all that white stuff?" asked 9 year old Nell, sticking her neck out the open window. For a mile all you could see on both sides of the dirt road was an expanse of white.

"That is called cotton", answered Willene. Thinking back to her younger years when Daddy grew cotton and being as young as 4 or 5 years old, having to pick cotton. The sight of these cotton fields were not a good memory!

"Do you eat it?"

"No, dear, it can be used for a lot of things. As a matter of fact, your dress is made from cotton."

"It doesn't look like cotton", as Nell surveys her dress and looks back at the fields of white, perplexed.

Nearing the home of her aunt and uncle, Willene sighs out loud, and holds back the tears. This is one of the hardest things she has had to do, but knows there is no other option at this time. She looks in the rearview mirror and eyes her two little sisters in the back seat. Pearlene, small for her age of 8 years, is asleep. She had slept for the majority of the trip from Macon. Her hair is matted from the intense heat of a typical summer day in Georgia.

The year is 1942. Willene is 24 years old. She has two other siblings; a brother and a sister. Morris is already married; Lois, the eldest, is also married and living in Florida. Naturally, it fell on Willene's shoulders to take care of these two younger siblings since the death of their Mother. She lived and worked in Macon. She had brought her two little sisters to live with her, but having to work so much of the time to make ends meet, she felt inadequate to continue this arrangement. Plus, she needed to move to Savannah for a better job opportunity that was awaiting her. What else could she do?

Their Mother, Pearl, died when Nell was 2 and Pearlene was a newborn. After their Mother passed away, the family stayed together for about five years. Lois had already married before Pearlene was born; Morris and Daddy didn't get along very well, so about the time she left for Macon, Morris had already moved out. He had gotten a job as a mechanic, and his boss was letting him live in a section of the business' garage. Daddy wasn't much help. He spent most of his time down at the liquor store. He had secured this job when he gave up on farming.

"Is that their house?" Nell pointed at a house in the distance, breaking Willene's train of thought.

"Yes, it is." As she spoke, Pearlene awoke startled. The car was bouncing around on the dusty dirt road, jostling the girls all around in the backseat. Trying to avoid potholes was almost impossible. The house looked foreboding as they rounded the last curve of the road.

Among the pine trees sat an old clapboard house. This was your typical backwoods abode in the poor countryside of south Georgia. No other house was around for several miles. The old house was badly in need of repairs; the roof was sagging, the boards on the sides of the house had never been painted, and the steps leading up to the front porch were rotted. This was truly a "working" farm.

Not only did Uncle Otis and Aunt Daisy grow cotton. Other crops grown were tobacco and peanuts. Never without a large garden for their vegetables, they also raised chickens and turkeys for their meat and eggs.

As Willene surveys the old farmhouse and its' state of disrepair, she questions herself again. Am I doing the right thing leaving my sisters here with my aunt and uncle? Their lives are going to change drastically from this day forward, and mine!

As the three disembark from the car, Aunt Daisy and Uncle Otis wave from the front porch. Aunt Daisy looks the part of a typical woman from the backwoods. Her attire is a stained, full-length apron covering her dress. Her premature gray hair is tied up in a severe knot on top of her head.

Her face shows signs of the hard life she has had as a child, and now raising five children while farming the land. She is an average size with ample hips that came in quite handy carrying babies around while working the farm. Her personality is one that puts everyone at ease. Easy to converse with, she has many friends and is respected in the community. Uncle Otis is a small man with a quiet demeanor. He has on overalls that are rolled up to compensate for his short legs. You never heard him raise his voice. Even when he talks, it wasn't much more than a whisper. They both are avid church-goers and profess Jesus as the Lord of their lives. They are a hard working couple that love each other, and are very charitable toward others.

Several chickens were running around the front yard. Nell and Pearlene were both scared of the chickens and their strange noises, and hid behind their sister's skirt. As they are standing there awaiting our approach, five heads poke out the front screen door.

"Hello Aunt Daisy and Uncle Otis, this is Quinelle, loosening Nell's grip on her skirt and pushing her front and center, "she is 9 years old now. And this is Pearlene," taking her hand and pulling her alongside Nell, "she is 8."

Aunt Daisy steps down off the porch and hugs each one of us. Uncle Otis follows suit. The kids at the door come out onto the porch and just stare. "It's been a long, long time," said

Aunt Daisy. "Welcome to our home. Come on up and meet our children, your cousins."

Uncle Otis made his way toward the car, "I'll get their bags." That didn't take long since they each had only one small suitcase and a few other belongings packed into a pillowcase.

Aunt Daisy put her arms around Nell and Pearlene, gathering them to herself. "Kids, this is Quinelle and Pearlene, Here's Georgia - she's your age, Pearlene. This is Bill," pointing at a tall, skinny boy, "he's 14 years old."

"This here is Harry," pointing at a chubby, round-faced boy. "Harry is 6 years old." Putting her arm around the smallest one, "This is Nick, our youngest. He is 2 years old. And, this one is the oldest, Margaret, she's 16." The children each nodded as they were introduced.

Georgia, excited about having someone nearer her age and a girl at that, grabbed Pearlene's and Nell's hands and said," I'll show you our bedroom. Come on!"

Margaret followed them in. "I'm coming, too."

Nick chimed in, "Me, too", slamming the screen door behind him.

"Come on in, Willene, let's get some lemonade. You too, boys," said Aunt Daisy. Uncle Otis brought the suitcases and pillowcase in and told Bill and Harry to take them to the girls' bedroom. As Aunt Daisy fixed the lemonades, and the children were getting acquainted, Uncle Otis said to Willene, "You are doing the right thing, you know. They will be just fine here with us. You have been a wonderful big sister to these two. They may not understand now why you seem to be abandoning them, but one day they will understand."

"Thanks for saying that," replied Willene as she hugged his neck. "I can do this because I know they will be in safe hands here. I will visit just as often as I can."

"You let me know if they need anything, and I'll do my best to get it to them. Nell..Quinelle...we have gotten in the habit of calling her Nell...and Pearlene, should have enough clothes to begin school next month. Write me if they need anything before my next visit in a couple of months."

"What exactly will you be doing in Savannah?" asked Otis.

"I will be in a training program for welding. This is a great opportunity for a woman in a man's world, meaning I can make more money doing this than anything else! If all goes well, I will be working in the shipyard. I wouldn't be able to take advantage of this opportunity if it weren't for the both of you."

While the three of them were sipping their lemonades, the children rush in with cries of "We're thirsty!" Pearlene and Nell clamor to sit in Willene's lap while Daisy pours the lemonade.

"How do you like your room?" Willene asked the girls.

Nell, sheepishly replies, "It's okay, me and Pearlene have one bed and the other bed is for them", pointing at Margaret and Georgia.

Daisy passes out fresh-baked cookies to the children. "Why don't you kids go out on the porch with your cookies and lemonade? It's probably cooler on the front porch than it is in this kitchen," prodding the children along.

The four girls head on out to the porch, with Nick right behind them. Bill and Harry saunter out, not especially crazy about being around all those girls! Bill whispers to Harry, "And I thought two sisters were bad enough!"

After conversing for another few minutes, Uncle Otis announces he has chores to do and must get busy. "There's always something to be done on a farm!" Otis heads out to the barn. He calls the boys to come and help him. Everyone works on a farm. Otis decided to let the girls visit for a while with their cousins.

"Aunt Daisy, you will find this out soon enough, but I thought I would tell you a little about the girls. Pearlene is quite the chatter box - I guess, you could say she's like me," Willene said with a slight chuckle. "Nell is the quiet one - like your sister was.

Aunt Daisy nodded in agreement.

"Nell has been doing really well in school. She's a good listener, and seems to crave learning new things. Pearlene does well, too, but she could do better if she listened a little more instead of talking. Also, Nell likes for things to be in order. "

"Well, that's a good thing. Maybe she will be a good influence for my girls."

"Also, Nell is very shy. It may take her a while to warm up to you and Uncle Otis. She is very protective of her little sister."

"Just like Pearl," Aunt Daisy reflected on the memory of her older sister. "Let's go to the porch and see if we can catch a breeze!"

Aunt Daisy and Willene move out to the rockers on the porch. "Sure is hot," exclaimed Aunt Daisy.

Nell's stomach was in knots. She knew it wasn't much longer that Willene would leave them. Willene had replaced the Mother that she didn't even remember. Why couldn't they go to Savannah with her? It wasn't fair.... life isn't fair. How can Pearlene play with Georgia and laugh? There is nothing to laugh about....

Chapter 2

"Well, I've got to head on back home. It's about a three hour drive back to Macon. I've got so much to do to get things ready to move the end of next week," Willene says as she gets out of the porch rocker and stretches and yawns. The girls have been sitting on the front porch steps mostly listening to the two adults' conversation sharing news of mutual friends and relatives, past and present. Daisy did a lot of reminiscing about her sister, Pearl, with Willene. She talked of how much she missed her, and was glad she could take care of her children, Nell and Pearlene.

Nell and Pearlene rise to their feet, and immediately grab Willene around the waist. They both knew it was time; a time that they both were dreading; and now it was here. Willene returned their hugs and said, "I'll be back to visit just as soon as I can. Ya'll mind Aunt Daisy and Uncle Otis. You will be happy here, I just know it. You will make new friends, and won't it be fun to have two more sisters?"

Nell and Pearlene nodded in agreement. "Walk with me to the car," Willene said to her sisters. As they approached the driver's side of the car, Willene told them, "I left Aunt Daisy my new address in Savannah. Write to me as often as you can, and I'll write to you. You will be a part of this family now. They will be good to you, and in time, you will learn to love them. Do as you are told. There will be chores for you, just like the other kids have. Everyone has to work on a farm. I know I've already told you this before we left home, but don't be lazy and let sadness get the better of you. Try to be happy. This is a new chapter in all our lives. Let's do and be the best we can be, okay?"

Unable to speak because of their crying, both Nell and Pearlene nodded while hugging Willene's neck. It was all Willene could do not to cry herself.

"Okay, girls, I've got to get going," as she climbs into the driver's seat. "I'll write you before I leave for Savannah next weekend. Look for my letter next week. I will miss you both so much, and just know that I love you!"

"Love you, too," the both of them said simultaneously.

Willene cranked up the old '37 Chevrolet, drove off waving good-bye to the little sisters she had practically raised by herself. They stood in the yard, waving frantically and blowing kisses. Aunt Daisy came to them, bent down, and wrapped her arms around the both of them, all the while wiping their tears away with the hankie she had pulled from her apron, "She'll be back soon for a visit, don't you worry. Let's go back in the house and have some more lemonade, and you can help me, Margaret and Georgia fix some supper."

As the dust arose from the dirt road, Willene, looking in her rearview mirror, watched as Aunt Daisy walked the girls back into the house. They were going to be all right, she reassured herself. Thank you, God, for strength to do this. She thanked God for taking care of her girls.

After the supper meal, Quinelle and Pearlene helped the girls clean up the kitchen. They were accustomed to cleaning up the dishes for Willene. But, now there are so many more dishes to clean up! Georgia and Margaret were talking about their last days of the school year they had just completed. They asked their cousins a lot of questions about their home and school in Macon. Quinelle didn't have much to say; Pearlene did most of the talking, as usual. Quinelle just wasn't in the mood.

How am I going to make it without Willene? Quinelle couldn't get Willene out of her thoughts. Aunt Daisy and Uncle Otis and her cousins all seemed very kind, but she still didn't want to be living with them. She wanted to go home. How could Willene abandon them like this? Quinelle and Pearlene held onto each other and cried softly together.

Chapter 3

I awoke with a start. Someone was crying. Then I realized the crying and the tears were my own. I turned toward *the picture window*. The curtains were drawn. I could tell it wasn't dark outside yet. Someone had drawn the curtains to keep the descending sun from streaming in the window. I enjoy watching the sunset when I am able to stay awake long enough.....

———

Moaning with pain in her body, Quinelle strained to change her position in the bed.

"Quinelle, are you okay?" asked Etheel, approaching her bedside.

Quinelle slowly nodded her head. "I would like for you to open the curtains so I can watch the sunset."

"All right. I can do that." While Etheel was drawing the curtains back, she asked, "Are you hungry? You really need to eat something. I made a fresh pot of chicken broth."

"Not feeling hungry at all, but I will try," she answered.

Etheel asked, "Are you in a lot of pain? I thought I heard you crying."

Quinelle replied with a sigh, "I woke myself up crying. I was remembering a time when I was a little girl. Willene had taken me and Pearlene to live with Aunt Daisy and Uncle Otis. It was a very sad time for me."

"Oh, speaking of Willene, she called a little bit ago while you were sleeping. She called to check in on you and told me to tell you that she loves you and hopes to come visit real soon," Etheel said. "I'm going to warm up your soup. Be right back."

"Thanks, Etheel," whispered Quinelle.

Quinelle was so appreciative of Etheel helping her out in her greatest time of need. Etheel is Pete's sister-in-law; married to Pete's brother, J.N. Pete is by my side as much as he possibly can. Etheel and J.N. live down the road, and she stops in every day to check on me, sometimes cooking us a meal. Pete's Mother, (everyone calls her MaMa) lives with us and she helps out as much as she is able. Pete's Dad, David, died a few years ago.

————

Watching the sunset is one of the few enjoyments left in my life. I haven't been out of the house in weeks now. I have lost so much weight and barely have the strength to move about. The doctors say I have only a few months left.

————

"Okay, lady, here's your soup. Let me help you sit up," Etheel says as she places the soup on a tray by the bed.

Getting situated to eat is quite an ordeal, but Etheel is strong and is able to sit me up in the bed without much effort on her part. She has to feed me. I don't have the stamina or strength to hold the spoon. She has been such a good friend to me all these years.

"I've eaten all I can right now," Quinelle said, as she turned her head indicating that fact. "I just want to sleep right now."

Etheel helped her get positioned for rest, and told her, "MaMa is here. Pete will be here in about an hour. He had a church meeting. I'm headed to the house. See you tomorrow."

"Thanks again," Quinelle said.

She was saddened to think that she had missed Willene's phone call earlier.

———

I really miss my sister. Sinking into the pillows, her body succumbed to the weariness that she felt in her bones, and the need to close her eyes and think of her younger and vibrant years.

Chapter 4

"Load up, kids," hollered Aunt Daisy, "we are ready to go."

All seven of us clamored into the bed of the old pick-up truck; Aunt Daisy and Uncle Otis in the cab. Tonight would be the first night in our new home in Uvalda, a small town a few miles from where we showed up at our cousins, the Clark family, two years ago. Uncle Otis had sold the farm, and had obtained a job with Watkin's Products. He will be a route salesman for surrounding communities. We are leaving behind those cotton and peanut fields for someone else to harvest! That was some hard work. Every day in the fall after we got in from school, we had to go straight to the fields and pick cotton before it got dark. My fingers have been bloodied from the pricks from pulling the cotton off their sharp stems. The hot sun was almost unbearable at times - even in the fall. That is something I won't miss.

We have been to our new home on several occasions in the process of moving. Family and friends pitched in, driving their trucks over and loading up our furniture and such. Our new house is quite smaller and closer to town. The best part is now we have running water inside the house and indoor plumbing. No more treks aside to the outhouse! We girls, Margaret, Georgia, Pearlene, and myself will still have to share a room, but that's okay. It won't be long before Margaret will finish high school, and she has already been asked to marry. Her beau is Levi, a tall, dark and handsome boy that likes to pick on us girls. He seems to be a sweet guy. He is 18 years old, and hopes he won't get drafted before they can get married. He is hoping the war will end before that happens. Well, anyway, when she gets married, there will be more closet space!

Aunt Daisy will still have a garden and some chickens. Nothing like gathering eggs in the morning for our breakfast!

Aunt Daisy has taught us girls how to cook by watching her and giving us free rein at times in the kitchen. She is very patient with us, and her goal is to prepare us for marriage. The best way to a man's heart is through his stomach, she would say.

She, also, takes time to show us how to sew and mend clothing. New clothes are a luxury around here. Everything we wear practically is home-made, not store bought. She has told me that she is going to teach me how to cut a dress from a pattern. She will have more time since the farm is no longer.

"Hey, Nell," Bill said, while nudging her gently, "you are daydreaming again! Whatcha thinking about? Your boyfriend?"

Nell retorted by sticking out her tongue at Bill. He knew she didn't have a boyfriend! He just liked to tease her, always telling her she was too skinny, and needed to fatten up; that guys liked girls with meat on their bones. Bill and I have gotten along pretty good these past two years. He was a few years older than me, but he was protective of me and Pearlene. We bantered back and forth a lot, just having fun. I am the quiet one and he's pretty boisterous! He could always make me laugh.

We finally arrived at our new residence. It was late in the day, and Aunt Daisy went directly into the kitchen to start supper. As the custom, we girls followed to help out in any way that she asked us to. It is so nice to have running water in the kitchen. We would take turns at our old house bringing in water from the well. That was a chore!

"What's for supper?" asked Harry.

"It's a surprise!" Aunt Daisy replied, "Now get out of here, out of our way. Go outside with your brothers. See if your Dad needs some help with anything."

"What IS for supper?" asked Pearlene.

"Same old, same old," Aunt Daisy said, "fried chicken, rice, beans, and biscuits. The surprise is.... while you girls are preparing the meal, I'm going to make some apple pies. You know sugar has been scarce since the rationing due to the war going on. Well, Otis was able to get us some sugar while in town yesterday. That will be our way of celebrating our new home."

"All right!" Georgia exclaimed.

The kitchen hummed with excitement. This new kitchen made preparing a meal seem less of a chore!

Tomorrow was going to be even better. Willene is coming to see us! I really do miss her! I can hardly wait!

After supper and apple pie we gather in our new living room for our nightly devotion and prayers. Uncle Otis began by reading scripture from the Bible. He then bowed his head, and we knew to follow his lead, and thanked God for our new home, and also for success in his new job. Afterwards, he and Aunt Daisy hugged all of us children, and we were told that we were loved. And, I felt it, too. Pearlene and I giggled uncontrollably under the covers of our bed.

"Ya'll better calm down. Momma and Daddy will hear you," warned Georgia from her and Margaret's bed located at the foot of their cousins' bed.

Margaret said, "Georgia, they are just excited because their sister, Willene, is coming to visit tomorrow. It's been a while since she has been here. How long has it been, Nell?"

Quinelle responded, "Almost three months. Her job is keeping her so busy. And, since gas is being rationed because of the war, she has not had the gas to travel. She told me and Pearlene in her last letter she is bringing us some new material so your Momma can make new dresses for school. I can hardly wait to see her. I wish tomorrow was here already."

15

"Me, too," chimed in Pearlene. "Maybe she will bring us a surprise like she usually does, you think, Nell?"

"I'm pretty sure she will," answered Quinelle.

"Well, tomorrow will get here sooner if we all go to sleep," Margaret chided, "now cut out the laughing and talking. Good night."

"Good night."

Quinelle hadn't been this happy in a while. She was actually laughing.

Chapter 5

Pearlene and Nell were in the kitchen cleaning up after breakfast when they heard a car drive up in the yard.

"She's here!"

They ran out of the house like it was on fire, straight into Willene's open arms. Willene had left really early to be able to spend practically the whole day with them. She would be leaving tomorrow since she had to be back at work on Monday morning. So, they only had one day to spend with her.

"Did you bring us a surprise, Willene?" Pearlene blurted out.

Willene just laughed and said, "Well, give me time to get in the house and see everyone. Then, I'll show you the material I bought for your new dresses, and just maybe there will be something else in that suitcase for you."

Uncle Otis, Aunt Daisy, and the kids rounded the corner from the back of the house where they were planting a fall garden.

"So good to see you, Willene," Aunt Daisy said as she hugged her neck. "These girls have been so excited."

Everyone exchanged hugs and greetings. Bill, the oldest boy, grabbed Willene's suitcase for her and took it into the girls' bedroom.

Pearlene and Nell could hardly wait for some time alone with Willene. Finally, the others went back to their chores. The three sisters were finally alone for a little while.

When seated on the bed in the girls' bedroom, Willene

opened the suitcase and laid out the new material for their new dresses.

They oohed and aahed over them. Also, were two new pairs of shoes. "I hope your feet haven't grown too much since spring," said Willene, "don't wear these until school starts next month."

The girls looked in anticipation at the suitcase that Willene was keeping to herself, so the girls couldn't peek in.

"Now the surprises," Willene announced. "Pearlene - for you - some doodle pads and new color pencils. I know how you like to draw." Digging back into the suitcase, Willene, presented a book to Quinelle. "This is a brand new book that I know you will just love. A movie was made from this story - Gone With the Wind." Quinelle hugged the book to her chest. Books were a luxury and she did love to read. This book would take a long time; it was the biggest book she had ever seen.

"Thanks, I love my pads and color pencils," Pearlene said as she hugged Willene's neck.

"Thank you for my book."

"You're both welcome," Willene said as she returned their hugs. "Now, I have some news. I received a letter from Daddy."

Quinelle butted in, "Is he coming to see us? We haven't seen him in a few months."

Willene continued, "Do you remember your Uncle Otis' sister, Cornelia?"

The girls both nodded.

"Well, your Dad and Cornelia were married a couple of weeks ago."

They looked at each other in astonishment. "Does this mean we have a new momma and will go and live with them?" Quinelle asked.

"No, you both will still live here." Willene answered.

"Oh, they doesn't want us, right?" Quinelle said with a downcast look.

"I don't want to leave here anyway," Pearlene said with her arms crossed against her chest. "I like it here."

"So do I," said Quinelle.

"Daddy said he will probably be around to see you both in a week or so." Willene quickly got up, closed the suitcase, indicating that was the end of that conversation. "Okay, let's go into town and get us an ice cream cone." She didn't have to say it but once, and the girls were headed for the car.

Chapter 6

Willene left the next morning for Savannah. Aunt Daisy had prepared a huge breakfast, making sure Willene ate before she left. We said our sad good-byes, with Willene promising to write next week.

Sundays were our day of rest. Uncle Otis did not allow any work to be done on Sunday, except for cooking and cleaning up the kitchen, and of course, attending church. We had plenty of time to get ready for church services on Sunday because Sunday School and church were not held until 1:00 in the afternoon. Most of the parishioners had to come from several miles around, and their only mode of transportation was a mule and buggy. Those of us who lived closer to the church would return on Sunday evenings for worship services that began at 6:00 p.m.

We would spend our Sunday mornings playing games or reading. Most of our time is spent outdoors, weather permitting. The house is small for nine of us. So, we have to plan ahead when having to all get ready at the same time! There was only one bathroom, but that was great compared to our facilities at the last house, which were outside! No time to dilly-dally when you got your turn!!

We attend the Uvalda Church of God - every Sunday. No ifs, ands, or buts. I like going to see the friends I have made there. Sunday School is really a lot of fun. I don't get much out of the preaching part, though. The preacher is loud and scares me sometimes.

Aunt Daisy and Uncle Otis have been members of this church since they married. They are involved in the church, always doing something. Aunt Daisy even plays the piano. She can't read music, but plays by ear. Georgia, Pearlene and Quinelle, on occasion, sing in church as a trio while Aunt Daisy plays. It is a very small church with just a few families that attend regularly besides the families of Clarks and Yeomans (that's Quinelle and Pearlene); there are the Mannings, the Stokes', and the Casons, to name the largest families that attend. We children are in one Sunday School class with exception of those 3 years and younger.

Those boys in the Stokes' family are aggravating and always picking on each other and us girls instead of paying attention while in Sunday School class. Nathaniel, who is also called J.N., and one of his brothers, Furman, are the worst of the bunch. Quinelle is very fond of their sister, Betty, who is a few years older than her. She is always kind to Quinelle. Furman is closest to her age. She's eleven and he is thirteen. He is kind of cute, Quinelle thinks to herself.

Harry jabs Quinelle in the side, and leans over and whispers "Are you daydreaming again?"

She jabs him back and rolls her eyes at him. They get the 'evil-eye' from Aunt Daisy. They know what that means! The children were taught to be still in church and absolutely no talking. But, she couldn't stop Quinelle from daydreaming.

Chapter 7

I open my eyes. The curtains on *the picture window* have been drawn again. I hear voices in the house.

———

Pete bends down over her bedridden body, takes her hand, and whispers, "I'm back from my meeting. Are you up for a visit from the Pastor?"

"I guess so. Help me sit up and comb my hair first," Quinelle requested.

Pete wrapped his arms under her armpits and pulled her up into a sitting position. He got her brush that was always nearby, and lovingly brushed her hair. The Pastor had been asked to remain in the kitchen until he was summoned.

A few minutes later Pastor McKinney entered the living room and proceeded to Quinelle's bedside. "I won't stay long. Just wanted to say hello and give you some news about the church library."

"What about the church library?" Quinelle asked with a startled look. This library had been her "baby." Over the years she had accumulated a large selection of inspirational and devotional books along with listening tapes. She wanted to share this collection with her church, and decided to set up a library where the books and tapes could be borrowed.

"Ella Martin has volunteered to oversee the books and

media you have obtained and donated for our library. She will follow up and make sure the books and tapes the members of the church borrow will get returned. We all appreciate your efforts and time pulling this together for our church," said Pastor McKinney.

"Oh, that's wonderful of her to do this for our church. That's such a relief to me. I know that Ella will do a great job," replied Quinelle.

"Anything I can do for you?" asked the Pastor.

"Just pray for me, please, before you leave."

"Certainly. I want you to know that at the conclusion of our meeting tonight, we prayed for you then." The Pastor then proceeded to take Quinelle's hand, placed his hand over hers, and asked God to ease her suffering, and if it be God's will, to heal her from this cancer.

———

Pete sits beside me on my bed, not ours. I wish I were upstairs in our bed. He tells me all about the meeting he attended at church this evening. Things are going great so far as our church is concerned. New members are being added and the church's finances are in good order. He tells me good night and that he loves me, and will check on me later. I tell him the same. He heads up the stairs to our bedroom.

Loneliness overwhelms me once again......................

Chapter 8

"Pearlene, are you awake?" whispered Quinelle to Pearlene.

"Yeah, what's wrong?" she answered.

"I still can't believe Willene is married! It's such a surprise. She never mentioned a Charles Fulghum before!" exclaimed Quinelle.

"Well, it's about time, don't you think? After all she is 29 years old," Pearlene retorted.

"I guess I'm happy for her, it's just......"

"Just, what?"

"She probably won't come to visit us anymore," Quinelle said with a cynical tone of voice.

"But, she did say in her letter that she would send us bus fare to visit them in Savannah for a week this summer," Pearlene reminded her.

"It just won't be the same," Quinelle replied, turning her back to the wall.

Quinelle silently cried as Pearlene dozed back off to sleep. Things would never be the same. She had lost her Mother, Daddy didn't come around much, and now, her sister. She felt abandoned again. That lonely feeling once again crept up on her. She shuddered from the tears. She didn't want to wake the others in the bedroom. Even with her baby sister, cousins and her Aunt and Uncle, she still felt so alone at times.

Willene had sent them a little money. Times were still hard for the Clark family; even with her cousins, Margaret and Bill out of the house now. Willene still sent Uncle Otis money to help with expenses. Quinelle decided she was going to get a ride into town the following weekend and pick out new material and make herself a nice Sunday dress, even may have enough left over for a new pair of shoes. She can now make her own clothes. Aunt Daisy had taught her how to sew.

She loved sewing, and she was pretty proficient at it. Pearlene wanted a store-bought dress. That would mean a trip into either Vidalia or Mt. Vernon, as Uvalda had no dress shops.

She wondered what Charles was like. Would he like them? Willene had said in her letter that he was in the Air Force stationed there in Savannah. She said that he was a perfect gentlemen and a very quiet, laid-back person. Willene didn't know how long they would remain in Savannah, but probably would know this summer, if and where Charles would be transferred some time the latter part of this year. That is really the part that disturbs her. What if Willene moves far, far away? What would she do without Willene being at least in the state of Georgia? She didn't want to think about that. She couldn't bear that thought just now. Too overwhelming.

Chapter 9

"Just think, next year we will be in the 10th grade!"

Quinelle and three of her friends from high school met at the end of the last day of their freshman year of high school at Big Martin's drugstore in Uvalda. They decided to splurge on an ice cream cone, as was their celebratory ritual for birthdays and special accomplishments. These friends were her closest and dearest since attending Uvalda Jr. High School. She didn't actually meet Etta Mae until ninth grade at Mt. Vernon-Ailey High School. Uvalda didn't have a high school; they had to be bussed to the nearby town of Mt. Vernon. Janelle and Christine were great friends of Quinelle's. The three attended Sunday school together. Etta Mae was really the closest friend - her confidant. She felt she could tell Etta Mae anything.

"Hey, Quinelle," Mr. Martin interrupted the girls, "Are you still looking for a part-time job this summer?"

Quinelle looked up at Mr. Martin (everyone called him Big Martin because he was a big man!), with a surprised look on her face, "Yes, sir I am."

"Your Uncle Otis was in the other day and let me know you wanted to work this summer. He said you could work part-time, not full-time. He told me how smart you are. I got to thinking and I could use someone on Fridays and Saturdays. What do you think?"

"Really?" Quinelle was not aware that Uncle Otis had

said anything to Mr. Martin. She had mentioned to her un-cle that she wanted to make some money this summer. He had agreed she could try to get a job, but only part-time. He, also, would make sure she would have a ride into town and back.

"Yes, do you want the job?"

"I would like that very much," Quinelle stammered. "When did you want me to start?"

"When can you start?" asked Mr. Martin.

"My sister and I are leaving this Saturday for Savannah to visit our older sister and her husband, but we will be back next Thursday. I could start the next day on Friday." Quinelle explained.

"Sounds good! Be here that Friday, say, 10:00?"

"I'll be here. Thanks so much!"

Big Martin left to wait on some customers. This was too good to be true. Maybe now she could have some money to help pay for piano lessons she desperately wanted to take her senior year. When the church got a new piano, Aunt Daisy asked if she could have the old upright. Aunt Daisy had shown me the basics, but she couldn't read music. I wanted to read music, but piano lessons were a luxury. I knew better than to ask.

"You got quiet, Nell. Whatcha thinking? nudged Janelle.

"She's thinking about that Furman Stokes, I bet," Christine teased.

"No, I was not. Was thinking about how I'm going to spend the money I'm going to make this summer," Quinelle retorted.

"What's this about Furman Stokes?" Etta Mae looked quiz-zically at Quinelle.

"You should see them at church. I can tell they like each other," said Janelle.

"Really? Nell, are you holding out on me?" Etta Mae laugh-ingly goaded her.

Quinelle sheepishly grinned. "Well, we talked after church

last Sunday night. He asked if he could see me sometime other than at church."

"I thought he was seeing Betty Jo?" Christine said as she spun around on her stool at the ice cream counter.

"I think they broke up."

"Well, what did you tell him?"

"I said that would be okay, but would have to check with my Uncle."

"When were you planning on telling your 'dear' friends about this? How could you keep this from us?" The girls were giggling.

"Today. I was going to tell you today." Quinelle then laughed right out loud, which was not her style. She was often told she was too serious, and needed to laugh more. Maybe Furman Stokes could help her with that.

Chapter 10

Our visit with Willene and her new husband, Charles, was a lot of fun. They took us sightseeing around Savannah. It is a beautiful city. We had never seen anything like this before. The biggest city we have been to is Vidalia; and it's nothing compared to Savannah! Charles was very sweet to us. He is very handsome, and seems to love our sister very much. She deserves someone to love.

Their apartment is very quaint, and right in the heart of downtown Savannah. It is very small, but does have two bedrooms. Willene has painted the walls a pale blue throughout the apartment. It is very cheery and comfortable. We are so happy for her. It is so good to see her this happy.

"Now, tell me what is going on with you two," Willene asked as they prepared the supper meal while Charles was resting after coming in from work.

Pearlene spoke up first, "I'm really excited about going to high school next year. I will be in the same school, finally again, with Nell. Georgia and I hope to get some of the same classes together. But, this summer, she and I have volunteered to help out in Vacation Bible School at the church. That will take a whole week up. We don't know yet what else we will be doing, besides working in the garden. I wish I could get a job like Nell, but Uncle Otis says no, that I'm not old enough yet."

"What job do you have, Nell? And, this is okay with Uncle Otis?"

"I'll be working in Big Martin's drugstore on Fridays and Saturdays during the summer. I'm hoping when school starts, he will let me continue to work Saturdays. I start next Friday."

"Well, that's wonderful. How much is he going to pay you?"

"I don't know yet. I'm sure it won't be very much, but it's better than nothing. I need some money."

"What do you need money for?" asked Willene

"I want to take piano lessons during my senior year, and Aunt Daisy says there just is not enough money to pay for them."

"Yeah, you ought to hear her banging on that old piano in the house," Pearlene commented.

"I wish I could help you out, Nell, but things are really tight for us, too. I send money already to Uncle Otis to help out with your expenses," Willene said as she gently caressed Nell's shoulder.

"I know that, Willene. Don't worry about it. I'm so excited about this job."

"That ain't all she's excited about?" Pearlene said with mischief in her eyes.

"What is she talking about, Nell?"

"Well.......A boy at church that I've known for a long time has asked to date me," Nell reported with a little grin on her face.

"What's his name?"

"Furman Stokes. He's wanting to come over to our house when we get back home and visit. I haven't talked with Uncle Otis about it yet."

Willene looked thoughtfully at Nell. "Well, you're not a child anymore. I'm sure if Uncle Otis knows his family from church, he will be okay with that."

"You think so?" Nell asked eagerly.

"I really think so!" Willene hugged Nell and Pearlene's necks. "I'm so glad you two are here."

Willene informed us at the onset of our visit that she had good news for us. Charles was not being transferred.

His orders were to remain in Savannah. Needless to say, we were overjoyed. Laughter comes easier now.

Chapter 11

Furman sat nervously on the couch between Quinelle and Harry. Furman had been invited to supper with the family, and was hoping to spend some quiet time with Quinelle. As a matter of fact, he was surrounded by the whole Clark clan seated in the living room.

"Where did your brother, Lamar, move after he got married? He's the oldest, right?" asked Otis.

"Right after they got married, he went off to war. When he got back home, they moved to Savannah," replied Furman, "They now have three daughters."

"What does he do for a living?"

"He works for Bankers Health and Life Insurance."

"Did your sister, Betty, move to Savannah, too, after she got married?" piped in Aunt Daisy.

Furman shook his head, "No, ma'am, she and her husband, Robert, are living somewhere outside of Warner Robins, a place called Cochran Field. It's not far from the Air Force Base there. She just had a baby girl."

The chatter continued for another half hour. Talk was mostly about Quinelle's new job and the new theatre in town.

"I better not catch any of you at the movies!" Otis reprimanded the children, with his finger wagging at them. "It's an evil thing that has come into our community. They call it progress." No one said a word for what seemed an eternity. Everyone just looked at the others.

"Okay, kids, it's 8:15 - time for devotion and to get ready for bed. Furman, you can stay for our Bible-reading."

"It won't be long tonight - just five minutes or so, but you must leave by 9:00," Otis announced as he proceeded to pick up the large Bible on a nearby table.

"Okay," replied Furman.

The next few minutes Furman listened as Otis read from the Bible - a familiar scripture - Psalm 23. Then, they all bowed their heads as Otis prayed aloud thanking God for taking care of them, and to bless the service at church tomorrow, and that souls would be saved.

As the children said good night and traipsed off to their rooms, Otis reminded Quinelle that Furman must leave the house by 9:00 sharp.

"Good night, Furman, see you in the morning at church," Daisy said as she headed to the kitchen for last minute preparations for tomorrow's breakfast.

"Good night, Mrs. Clark, and thanks for supper," Furman replied.

"Good night," Otis said as he headed to his bedroom.

Finally, Furman thought, I have Quinelle all to myself for 15 minutes, according to the clock on the wall.

"Why did you quit school?" asked Quinelle after he had confided in her that he had dropped out.

"Just didn't like it, I guess. Too much time spent getting there and back since our house is in the Brewton-Parker school district. Maybe, if I was in your school, I would have stayed," Furman grinned sheepishly. "Besides all that, Daddy needs me on the farm."

"I want to go to college so badly, but I just need to 'put that out of my mind' says Uncle Otis. There's no money for that. My sister, Willene - you know, you met her at church a couple of times when she came to visit - she can't help. She's married now....well, anyway, I'm hoping I can take piano lessons during school this coming year. At least, that's something!" Quinelle announced triumphantly.

"I've got a question for you. I heard your Momma call you Pete at church the other day. Is that a nickname?" Quinelle asked.

"Yea, she calls me 'Pete' and calls my younger brother, Freeman 'Coot'."

"What do you want me to call you - Furman or Pete?" Quinelle asked teasingly.

"You can call me Pete. I think I would like that."

The few minutes they had together were gone too quickly. She walked him to the door and they said their good nights to one another. He climbed into the old Model A his Dad let him borrow, and headed the five miles to home.

Quinelle made her way quietly to the bedroom with a grin on her face. She really liked him. He was handsome, too. He had made her laugh. She would call him Pete.

Chapter 12

"Good morning, sweetheart," Pete whispered to Quinelle, as he opened up the curtains on *the picture window*. "Look how beautiful it is outside."

She slowly opened her eyes and saw the beauty of the dogwoods in bloom and the beautiful blue skies. She smiled and remembered what she had been thinking about. She laughed out loud.

"What are you laughing about?" Pete asked as he helped her to sit up on the side of the bed.

"I was just thinking about our first date. You were so awkward around Aunt Daisy and Uncle Otis, and I was so nervous."

"Remember when Uncle Otis would shout out - "it's 9:00 - bedtime!"

Pete hugged her and held her hand. The memories were flooding in. He laughed. "We had some good times, didn't we - even as poor as we were."

She nodded as Pete stood up and announced, "I'm going to the kitchen and fix you some breakfast and you'd better eat it."

"I'll try my best."

"I know you will, you always do- that is, try your best. You were, and are, such an inspiration to me. You've always inspired others to do their best and be their best." With that said, he headed to the kitchen.

I love that man! I am so thankful God gave him to me. We have had a great life together.

I am so exhausted. I hate this. I want to be outside tending to my flowers. This is my favorite time of year. I remember always helping Aunt Daisy to plant a garden each spring. She knew how much I wanted to grow a flower garden, so finally, one spring, she bought me some flower seeds. Flower seeds were a luxury - you can't eat flowers. With the money I was making from the drugstore, I was buying my own material now to make mine and Pearlene's dresses. This was Aunt Daisy's way of showing her appreciation for my helping out and for good grades. Uncle Otis never said a word about it.

I'm probably going to miss the birthday dinner this year. For so many years now the Uvalda community has celebrated Aunt Daisy's birthday the 4th Sunday in June. Aunt Daisy and Uncle Otis were pillars of the community. I don't know exactly how the celebration started, but every year people in the community came together after church, (of course,) and brought food for lunch. Lots of food! The dinner was held in the community house in Longpond, a small community outside Uvalda city limits to be able to accommodate the number of people that came. We all sang happy birthday to Aunt Daisy. I always enjoyed traveling to Uvalda to see my cousins and friends throughout the years.

I snuggle back under the covers praying for God's divine will. I believe God loves me. I have never doubted that. Church members and my family are praying that I will be healed. I feel a little weaker each day, but am still trusting God to heal me. I know He can if it's His will. I've seen people healed in revival meetings. He still heals today.

Like a daisy, picking off its' petals one by one - He will heal me....He won't heal me....He will heal me......

Chapter 13

"He loves me...he loves me not....He loves me......."Quinelle sings happily as she picks the petals off one of her daisies.

"Let's go," said Uncle Otis, "or you'll be late for work."

Quinelle put down what was left of the daisy and ran to get into the car. Uncle Otis usually took her into work every Saturday. Saturdays were her favorite day. Not only did she enjoy her job, but she would get to see her handsome beau.

She and Pete had been dating for a little over a year now. They had three dates every week. Pete would come by the house every Thursday for supper and could stay until 9:00. Then, every Saturday, he would treat her to supper when she got a break from the drugstore. They would go to the corner diner and have their usual - a hamburger and a coke each. Pete's Dad would give him fifty cents on Saturday mornings for his help during the week on the farm. This meal took all of his fifty cents! Then, they would see each other at church. After church services which were held early afternoons, Pete would borrow his Dad's truck and they would go for long drives around the county until time to go back to Sunday evening church service. Their conversations had turned to more serious matters. They were now discussing marriage and how many children they wanted.

"Can you believe this is my last year of school?" Quinelle prattled on as she took a seat in "their" booth at the diner. "Oh, Aunt Daisy told me last night that the school board voted that all students must now attend twelve years of school to graduate. Thank goodness, this doesn't go into effect until next school term. I just made it. I get to graduate after this year - the eleventh. Pearlene and Georgia weren't too happy about it. They are in the tenth grade, so they will have to go two more years instead of one. I think it's funny."

"Well, that's great for you.... and us!" Pete exclaimed as he put in their order for the hamburgers and cokes.

"What do you mean, us?" She pretended like she didn't know what he was talking about.

"You know... you and me....getting married after you graduate."

Quinelle sank back into the booth and didn't say anything.

"You still want to marry me, don't you?" Pete asked with alarm in his voice.

"Yes, but have you thought about the details of getting married?"

"What do you mean, the details?"

"For one thing, how are you going to support us?"

"Well, I will still be helping my Dad out on the farm. You know since Nathaniel and Etheel married, it's just my younger brother, Coot, and me to help out. Nathaniel is working in the pulpwood business and Coot is too young to operate the farm machinery. I sometimes peel bark off the pine trees for the county for their electric poles. They pay pretty good wages. I have done some carpentry for Mr. Wolf, whom my Dad leases farmland from. I even built our outhouse!" He announced proudly.

"Where would we live?"

"I don't know yet. We've got time to figure that out."

Pete went to the counter to pick up their supper. Quinelle did want to marry Pete, but still had that nagging desire to go to college. She hadn't given up on the idea, but no one had given her any reason to hope, except her English teacher, Mrs. Holland. She encouraged her to go, telling her she would be good college material, with her good grades and brains. But, there was no way that this was going to happen. She couldn't even afford piano lessons anymore. It took all she made on Saturdays at the drugstore to pay for her school lunches, material for her clothes she made, and a few toiletries she needed. She didn't spend money on make-up; wearing make-up was strictly forbidden by her Aunt and Uncle. The church taught against it, too. I guess that's why movies are forbidden, too. All that make-up the actresses wear!

"Here's our food, Quinelle."

They ate in silence noting they had only a short time together. Pete wanted to have more time with Quinelle. He wanted them to get married just as soon as she graduated. He would trust God to help him to find a way to convince her that he could take care of her.

After finishing their burgers, Pete slid his arm around Quinelle, and said, "I love you, Quinelle and want to marry you." He then gave her a peck on the cheek.

She pulled away quickly, "Don't do that! Someone may see you."

He just laughed. She was so sweet and pretty. He couldn't help himself.

Quinelle nudged him out of the booth and said, "Look at the clock. I've got to get back to work. I don't like to be late."

"I'll pay the check, you wait here."

She waited for him to walk her back to the drugstore, as was his custom every Saturday evening. She had three more hours to work.

"I'll see you at church tomorrow," as he waved good-bye at the entrance of the drugstore, with a silly grin on his face.

She thought to herself as she returned his wave, and wondered what it would be like to be married to Pete Stokes?

She smiled and laughed a lot more these days. Georgia told her she did.

Chapter 14

It was a cold, blustery day in January. Pete had borrowed his Dad's truck for his weekly Thursday night visit to Quinelle. Halfway to her house, the rain started coming down in sheets, and the wind was blowing fiercely. If his Dad had known the weather was going to turn this ugly, he wouldn't have allowed him to take the truck.

Quinelle was in the kitchen helping with the preparations for supper. She was afraid Pete wouldn't make it tonight. She was concerned about his safety, but at the same time would be so disappointed if he didn't make it for her birthday celebration. He had told her last Sunday at church that he had a surprise for her. The suspense was killing her!

"I see headlights," Harry announced from the living room.

Quinelle ran to the front window to see the old truck pull up into the yard. By the time Pete got into the house he was drenched.

"Get by the fire, Pete," Uncle Otis said as he poked the burning firewood.

"Georgia, set another place at the table. Everyone wash up. Supper's almost ready." Aunt Daisy expected everyone to be seated around the table within the next five minutes after she made her announcement that supper was ready. That was the rule.

After a fine supper of fried chicken, butterbeans, mashed potatoes and biscuits, everyone exited to the living room with the exception of Pearlene and Georgia, who stayed behind in the kitchen for clean-up duty. They swapped out other duties with Quinelle as to allow her to spend time with Pete on Thursday nights. That was the deal!

Before the girls could complete their clean-up in the kitchen, Aunt Daisy told them to go ahead and bring out the birthday cake.

It was a school night and they needed to go ahead with the birthday celebration. Pearlene placed a single candle in the center of the pound cake and presented it to Quinelle. Aunt Daisy headed to the piano and pounded out "Happy Birthday" as everyone sang.

"Now, make a wish, Nell," Georgia said.

"I bet I know what she is wishing for!" teased Harry.

Quinelle blushed. Harry was always teasing her about Pete. She knew what he meant.

After blowing out her candle, Georgia and Pearlene presented Quinelle with a gift. It was a knitted throw they had worked on together. It had taken several months since they could only work on it when Quinelle wasn't around. It was Quinelle's favorite color - orange.

"Thanks so much," as she hugged the both of them, "I love it. This will certainly help keep me warm."

"Here's a little something from me and your uncle," Aunt Daisy said as she handed the gift to Quinelle. "Oh!" Quinelle exclaimed as she unwrapped her present of stationery and envelopes, "Thanks so much!" Now she would have something other than notebook paper when she wrote Willene. The stationery had flowers around the border. Perfect.

"Okay, everyone eat their cake and then on to the living room for our devotional," Uncle Otis said.

After cake, clean-up, and the devotional, everyone scattered but Pete and Quinelle. They had about 30 minutes left to be alone.

"Good night, Pete and Nell." Her Aunt and Uncle exited

the room. Uncle Otis turned around and reminded Pete that bedtime is in 30 minutes.

"Yes, sir," Pete replied.

Pete turned to Quinelle on the couch, "I didn't want to give you your gift until everyone was gone."

He then slipped his hand into his jacket and brought out a small box. "Sorry, I couldn't afford the wrapping paper."

"No bother about that," she assured him as she opened up the box.

"I just want you to know that I will love you for all time."

Inside was a beautiful Bulova wristwatch. She had never owned a watch. She immediately placed it on her wrist and exclaimed, "I love it, Pete." She gave him a quick peck on his cheek. "Oh, I get it, 'you will love me for all time' - you're so funny, Willie Furman."

"I should have never told you my full name."

"Nothing's wrong with your name, but I do prefer Pete."

Pete looked at the clock on the wall, ticking away the minutes. He had so much to talk with her about.

"Quinelle," he started, "I've got some news. I received a letter from my brother, Lamar, who lives in Savannah. He suggested that after you and I get married that we move to Savannah, and I could work for the company that he works for - Bankers Health and Life Insurance Company - they will be doing some hiring probably by the end of this summer. What do you think?"

"Savannah? That is where Willene and Charles are living!" She couldn't believe it - never in a million years did she think she would live anywhere but in Uvalda.

"I thought you might like that; but what would Daddy do without me to help out on the farm? I wanted to talk with you first before I mentioned this to Daddy."

"What would your job be?" Quinelle asked.

"Lamar called it a 'debit route' - don't know exactly what that is - but I would be collecting life insurance premiums."

"Bedtime!" Uncle Otis called out from his bedroom. This was the usual routine; Uncle Otis would call out that it was bedtime, and they knew they must immediately obey.

"We'll talk about this some more on Saturday, okay?" Pete took her hand and brushed his lips across the back of her hand. They stood up, he held her ever so gently, and kissed her quickly on her lips.

She walked him to the door. The rain had stopped, but the bitter cold air entered the room as she opened the door.

"I love you, Quinelle."

"I love you, too, Willie Furman," she said with laughter in her voice.

He wagged his finger in her face, then zipping up his jacket, turned to brave the 'oh-so cold' weather.

He watched her as she went inside, turning down the lights as she went to her bedroom. One day.....he thought. He was so excited about the prospect of being able to hold her all night long. He breathed a big sigh.....Thank you, Jesus, for putting Quinelle in my life.

Quinelle quietly climbed into bed. She now had Margaret's bed - since she was the oldest. Georgia and Pearlene now shared the other bed in the room. Seventeen - I'm finally seventeen, and only four months before graduation. Just thinking about the possibility of moving to Savannah, where she would be near Willene, was making her giddy. That wasn't all, either, that was making her giddy, as she quietly giggled to herself. She kept the wrist watch on, vowing never to take it off except to bathe. She knew he couldn't afford a ring, but that was okay. The watch was really more practical, anyway. And, I am a practical-kind-of-girl, so I've been told.

Chapter 15

This was to be their last time in Sunday School and church service at the Uvalda Church of God. Quinelle and Pete had told everyone that they were to be married the following Thursday, and then heading to Savannah right after the ceremony. Yes, Aunt Daisy and Uncle Otis had given permission for her to marry. Aunt Daisy had agreed to take them to the courthouse in Mt. Vernon. "I'm going to miss you so much, Nell," Pearlene sobbed as she hugged Nell's neck.

"Me, to," said Georgia, joining in on the hug.

Pearlene continued, "I'm so happy for you, Nell. Write us as often as you can. I'll see you next summer when I come to Willene's."

"That will be great, especially since I found out that our apartment in Savannah is very close to Willene's. We will have so much fun!"

The three girls were making their way out to the car with all of Quinelle's belongings. "I'll miss you both so much. I'll even miss Harry!" she commented with laughter. Harry was not at the send- off. He had already left for the hardware store where he worked.

As the girls were chattering, Mr. and Mrs. Stokes, Coot, and Pete had driven up. Pete was transferring his belongings to the trunk of Aunt Daisy's car.

"You got everything?" Pete asked Quinelle as he put her suitcase into the trunk.

"Yes, that's everything - everything I own!" Quinelle replied as they looked at one another with anticipation of what was to come.

Uncle Otis and Aunt Daisy shook hands with Pete's parents, David and Lucille. "See ya'll at church Sunday."

Uncle Otis hugged Quinelle, "Take care of yourself and just know that I love you." He shook Pete's hand and said, "Take care of my girl, you hear?"

"Yes, sir, " Pete answered as if addressing a drill sergeant. The three climbed into the car, waving good-bye to everyone as they backed out of the yard.

"I love you, son, " Lucille called out to Pete.

"Love you, and you, too, Daddy," Pete shouted out the open window. "And, Coot, help your Daddy!"

Pete was concerned about his Daddy. How was he going to take care of the farm with only his younger brother, Coot, to help? Coot is sixteen now, but doesn't have much experience with the farm machinery. That's a lot of work for just the two of them. He tried not to think about all that right now; this day was a very important day. He and his sweetheart were getting married today. His brother, Nathaniel and his wife, Etheel, were going to meet them in Mt. Vernon at the courthouse, and drive them to Savannah.

Quinelle couldn't believe this day had finally come. She had graduated with honors in May. It is now August 5th. Pete's job with Banker's Health and Life was not available to him until August 10th. They decided to continue working during the summer; she at Big Martin's and he on the farm, and any carpentry jobs he could get. They would save as much money as they could to purchase things needed for their new apartment.

Pete held Quinelle's hand as they traveled to Mt. Vernon. Aunt Daisy was chattering on and on, mostly about her church work. "The church is going to miss your singing, Nell, with Georgia and Pearlene. No more trio now, just a duet." She said with a chuckle.

"They'll do just fine without me," Quinelle said.

"Lamar and his wife, Martha, have told me about a small church they are attending in Savannah. It's a Pentecostal church, too," Pete volunteered this information to Aunt Daisy.

"That's good. Ya'll need to get in a good, Bible-based church," Aunt Daisy lectured. "That's important. Don't forget to read your Bibles every day, either."

Pete and Quinelle just smiled at one another. They were both looking forward to their new lives together, and that did include church. They had already discussed this with one another.

The ceremony took all of five minutes. The justice of the peace was all business. There were no rings to exchange; no money for that - yet; that would come later, say... in 10 years? – both would joke about that. Food and rent were foremost right now!

Aunt Daisy had to get back home, and left them sitting on the courthouse steps with all their wordly belongings in tow to wait for Nathaniel and Etheel.

"I wonder what our apartment looks like?" Quinelle was so excited about having a place of their own - no sharing a bedroom any longer except with her new husband. The bathroom was a different story. Pete had told her that they will be sharing a bathroom with two other couples in the apartment complex. She, also, knew the apartment was only two rooms total - one bedroom and a combination living and kitchen area. But, that didn't matter. She was Mrs. Pete Stokes, and that was all that mattered right now.

"I'm sure it will be okay. I trust Lamar's wife, Martha, when she told me that it was the best she could find already furnished, with our limited funds. Ten dollars a week for the rent is not too bad, I guess."

"It's so nice of her, too, to give us a couple of place settings and glasses. Aunt Daisy gave me a couple of her old cooking pots, and with the few things we have bought together, we have a good start, I think. Now, all we need is some groceries," Quinelle quipped as she held tightly to Pete's hand.

"Oh, also, Etheel told me last night they were going to give us a set of sheets for our bed and a some towels and wash-cloths as our wedding gift, so we don't have to go out and buy some like we thought we would. And.... Daddy handed me this as we were leaving the house this morning," as he pulled out a ten dollar bill from his pocket, "this will buy us some groceries until I get paid."

Just then, Nathaniel and Etheel drove up. The girls hugged each other.

"Are ya'll married?" Nathaniel questioned his brother as he slapped him on the back, nearly toppling Pete over.

"Yes, we are," Pete answered as he looked at his new bride with such gentleness. "Yes, she's all mine! Let me introduce you to Mrs. Quinelle Stokes."

Nathaniel and Etheel laughed at the gaiety of the new couple. He gave Etheel a 'knowing' wink!

"Let's get this show on the road, it looks like rain is headed our way," Nathaniel said as he and Pete picked up the suit-cases and bags, making their way to the car.

"Are ya'll hungry?" as Etheel indicated the bag of sand-wiches she had made before they left home that morning. "We can eat on the way."

"Sounds good to me," Pete said as they slid into the back seat. "Let's stop at that little store I saw on the corner and get us a bottle of pop. My treat."

Thus, began the life adventures of Pete Stokes and Quinelle Yeomans as husband and wife on August 5, 1950.

Chapter 16

I awake to the sound of rain pelting *the picture window*. The skies are gray now. The wind is howling. What time is it anyway?

Where's my watch? Is anybody here? All I can hear is the wind and rain. The curtains are still open, so it can't be too late.

Someone always draws the curtains when it's dark outside. What day is it? I keep losing track of what day it is. They all run together. I need someone to help me get up.

"Pete."

"I'm right here, Quinelle."

Pete gets out of a nearby chair and comes to my bedside. "You've been asleep a long time. Do you want to get up for a bit?"

"Yes, help me to the bathroom, please."

Pete leans over me and I wrap my arms around his neck. He lifts me up gently off the bed and carries me. I'm so weak. This is not what I expected or envisioned at 49 years of age. This can't be happening to me - to us. Oh, God, please either heal me or take me home.

Pete reminds me to be strong and keep believing for my healing. I'm trying - really trying, but this pain is too unbearable at times.

Thank goodness for the morphine that gives me some relief for a period of time, and helps me to rest.

Pete picks me back up and returns me to my hospital bed at the picture window. That's just a polite way of saying 'deathbed'.

I'd rather be here, though, than in the hospital. At least I can see out this window every day. It does help to calm me and think on better days.

I love to read, always have, but my eyes are too tired. I can't focus any longer. So, all I have left are the memories. At least, I can still remember.

As Pete lowers me back on the bed, I ask him to bring me some water.

"Anything else?" he patiently asked.

"No, just water. Is that MaMa I hear in the kitchen?"

"Yes, she wanted to fix supper tonight. Said she wanted to feel useful."

"That's sweet of her."

"I'll be right back."

The rain was pelting the picture window with a vengeance. I choke back the tears. I want more time......

"Here's your water," Pete says as he helps me to hold the glass. My hands are shaky.

Those talented hands, he thought. She could play a piano, could sew and crochet, cook up great meals, operate the adding machine and typewriter faster than anyone.

He knew she liked to talk about their early years together. She had been doing that a lot lately. "Any old memories rolling around in that head of yours today?"

"Why, yes. Earlier I was remembering the day we got married. Nathaniel and Etheel picked us up at the courthouse and were driving us to Savannah. Remember that downpour just as we were leaving Mt. Vernon, and it lasted the whole trip?"

"Yea, the windshield wipers weren't much help. Nathaniel had to drive about 25 mph for most of the trip.

"I thought we would never get there." Pete took the glass

of water from her. "The rain was coming down hard just like it is here now."

"I was already nervous thinking about our first time together, you know, as husband and wife." I squeezed Pete's hand. "I was scared that we might not make it to Savannah with the rain and all." The rain did stop just as we got into Savannah. We went to Lamar and Martha's place first, remember. Then, we followed them over to our new place."

"We were so thankful the rain had stopped. That made it much easier to unload our stuff. Remember, Quinelle, how Lamar and Martha had stocked our pantry for us that would help us out for the first couple of days, so we didn't have to go grocery shopping right away?"

"They were so good to us, weren't they?"

We continued to reminisce until MaMa (that's what the grandchildren call Lucille), announced it was suppertime.

"Pete, you and MaMa go ahead and eat. I'm not hungry just yet, anyway. When you get through, you can help me then. I'll try to get something down."

"Okay. I won't be long. We will be in the kitchen. Holler if you need anything."

I continue to think about that first day and night together as husband and wife. After his brothers and their wives left us alone, we were standing out on the sidewalk waving goodbye. We didn't know when we would see Nathaniel and Etheel again. After spending the night at Lamar's, they were heading back to Uvalda the next morning. All of a sudden, Pete picked me up, ran up the stairs to our apartment - it was on the second level - and carried me over the threshold.

Now, he picks me up and carries me so I can go to the bathroom. I can no longer hold back the tears.

Chapter 17

Pete's job with Bankers Health and Life was not his cup of tea. The hours were long and not much money; just enough to pay the rent and buy the groceries. He really needed more shirts and pants for this job. The ones he had were getting worn out for having to wash them so often! The city bus was the only way they had to get around town - to the laundromat and to the grocery store. They really enjoyed living in the city of Savannah. Quite different from Uvalda, to say the least. They took long walks - that didn't cost anything!

They attended the little church where Lamar and his family were members. Brother Poole was the pastor there. Not only did he pastor the church, but he built houses. Pastoring a church alone was not enough money to survive on.

Pete and Quinelle had been attending this church now for 3 months. On the way out of church this particular Sunday evening, Bro. Poole approached Pete, "How's your new job working out for you?"

"It's okay, I guess, it's a job," Pete answered.

"I hear you are pretty good at carpentry work. Your brother, Lamar, told me how you built the outhouse on your farm," the Pastor said while grinning ear to ear.

"Yes, I did."

Pastor Poole continued, "The building business in Savannah has picked up somewhat, and I could use some more help. Would you be interested?"

"Let me talk it over with Quinelle, but, yes, I am interested. Thanks so much." Pete, eagerly shaking the Pastor's hand, "I've been praying about this. I don't really like my job," he confessed.

"Can you let me know something Wednesday night when you come to church?"

"I will, for sure."

Pete hurried off to find Quinelle. She was already in the station wagon with Lamar's family. They usually got a ride to church with them.

"What was the Pastor talking to you about, Pete?" whispered Quinelle.

"I'll tell you when we get home." Pete didn't want to discuss it just now. He didn't know what Lamar would think about this offer from Brother Poole. Would Lamar understand if he resigned from his job at Bankers? After all, he was the one that recommended Pete for the job in the first place. He would talk with him tomorrow, but first we wanted Quinelle's opinion.

Once inside their little 'paradise', Pete surprised Quinelle by swooping her up in his arms and planting a big kiss on her lips. He put her down gently and said, "You won't believe this, but Bro. Poole has offered me a job helping him in his building business." What do you think about that?"

Quinelle knew he was not happy with his current job. He never complained to her about it, but she could sense in him a restlessness. He was used to getting his hands dirty, and she knew he missed that!

"It's whatever you want to do, sweetheart. I like Bro. Poole and I know he will treat you right and pay you a fair wage," she said as she slipped her arms around his neck.

They kissed for several moments, then Pete led her over to the sofa. The old springs in the sofa were so worn out, that they would literally sink almost to the floor. Quinelle leaned in against him and snuggled into his arms.

"I believe this could be the answer to my prayers, Quinelle.

I will talk with Lamar when he picks me up for work in the morning."

"I'm sure he will understand. He is concerned about your happiness, too."

Quinelle sat up. Heaving a contented sigh, "I am so happy here, darling. I'm so happy to be your wife. I love our little place here. I'm so happy to be near Willene. But, my happiness is not only about these things, but what I feel inside my heart. At the church in Uvalda, our preacher was so....how would you say it? Umm....staunch, and always talking about hell! Bro. Poole preaches more about the love Jesus has for us, and not about the things we must not do or we will go straight to hell for doing it!"

Pete laughed. He understood what she meant. He had been saved as a young boy while attending the church in Uvalda. That preacher had pretty much 'scared' him into making that commitment to Jesus. 'Saved' meant to him that he was 'saved' from hell! Through Bro. Poole's preaching, he now truly understood the meaning of being 'saved.'

Pete took her hands in his, "I was so happy that night a couple of months ago when you went down to the altar at church and told Bro. Poole that you realized that you needed to give your heart totally over to Jesus."

"Not only was it the Pastor's preaching that I realized there was more than just going to church and being good; it is you, Pete. You are so faithful each night to read the Bible and pray. I am so thankful to God that He brought us together."

He gathered her up onto his lap. She was so petite, all of ninety-five pounds, according to the drugstore weight machine - a perfect fit. They were a perfect fit, he thought. His heart swelled with so much love for her that his eyes glistened with tears.

"I love you so much, Quinelle Stokes," with brokenness is his voice.

"I love you, too, Willie Furman Stokes," she replied with a

hint of a tease. She knew what was on his mind other than this new job opportunity!

They nestled together in silence for the next few minutes. Pete knew in his heart that this job change was something he needed.

He had prayed and God had answered. Another chapter was unfolding in their lives.

Chapter 18

Pete began working with Bro. Poole after giving his two-week notice with Bankers. He never regretted making the change! He learned by watching his boss, and was taught the mechanics of homebuilding. Quinelle spent her days keeping a spotless home, (which didn't take much time!), trying out new recipes, reading and sewing. They had celebrated their first Christmas together. Pete had presented her with a sewing machine. She was totally surprised. She loved to sew, and had missed doing so. Pete told her this was not only her Christmas present but her birthday present, also, which was just a couple of weeks after Christmas. She, also, missed playing Aunt Daisy's old clunker of a piano, but she knew that it would be a long, long time before they could afford a piano! For Christmas Willene had given her a cookbook, *The American Woman's Cookbook*. It even had tips on how to save on groceries. She needed all the advice she could get. She was also enjoying listening to the radio that was given to them by Martha and Lamar. She had really missed listening to the music. There was never enough money for the luxury of a radio. They had decided, as a New Year resolution, to save as much as possible so they could buy a car. Pete was weary of depending on someone to get him to work, and if they had a car, Quinelle could take him to work, and she wouldn't have to take the city bus to run her errands any longer.

"There's a letter for you from your Momma," Quinelle told Pete as he hugged her after a long day on the construction site.

He tore the envelope open. He had been waiting for this letter, and hoping it would say what he wanted it to say. He decided he would sit down first before he began reading. Bro. Poole had told him a few weeks ago that he could use more laborers on his jobs.

Bro. Poole had contracted to build several houses, and he needed more laborers pretty quickly.

Pete had shared with Bro. Poole about his Father's plight to keep the farm going, and the many problems they were facing. Pete's Momma had told him that they had seriously been considering non-renewing their lease on the farm before spring planting began; but didn't know what they were going to do.

Bro. Poole said they could come work for him if they were 'to have a mind to move'. Pete had written his Dad, after talking with Bro. Poole, and asked would he and Coot be interested in working in construction. Of course, Pete had talked with his brother, Lamar, first to see what he thought about getting them to move. Lamar thought it was a great idea.

"Well?" asked Quinelle, as Pete silently read the letter.

"They're coming! Can you believe it? Momma and Daddy and Coot...here in Savannah and us working together?" Pete holding the letter out for her to read.

"That's wonderful, sweetheart, but it's hard to believe they are pulling up roots and moving. I am so surprised. I didn't think they would!" Quinelle said as she hugged Pete.

"Let's walk down to the corner drugstore and use the phone to call Lamar. I can't wait to tell him." Pete was beside himself with excitement.

"Your Momma probably sent a letter to Lamar, too, don't you think? Martha had told them to let her know if they decided to move, and she would start looking for a place for them to live."

"I want to call Lamar, anyway. Grab your coat."

"What about supper? It's almost ready!"

"Turn off the stove, we'll eat when we get back."

The January air was cold, but refreshing. Quinelle had been inside all day sewing, except for the quick trip down to the mailbox.

The day started with rain, but by mid-afternoon it had stopped, but remained cloudy. She had thought it would make for a good sewing day.

Back inside their apartment, they were shivering from the cold, damp air.

"Thanks for going with me, Quinelle," Pete gushed as he wrapped his arms around her. "I know you don't like the cold."

"Of course, I was going with you! Quinelle playfully pinched his cheek. "I can hardly wait for them to move - just think, they will be here in a month."

"We'll plan a party - invite Willene and Charles, Brother and Sister Poole and a few of our friends from church. Of course, we will have to have it at Lamar and Martha's house. You know, everyone could bring something, like we do at church - what do you call it?" Pete searching for the correct term.

"Potluck," Quinelle answered.

"Yeah, potluck. You could make some chicken and dumplings. Yours is the best!" Pete said as he finally let her go. "Woman, get my supper ready," he said as he patted her backside.

As Quinelle finished preparing the meal, Pete rested on the couch. He silently thanked God for answering yet another prayer.

Chapter 19

Quinelle was ectastic! Willene had just confirmed to her that she and Charles were expecting their first child. Now, there will be two newborns this year. Martha, Lamar's wife, was expecting her fourth child in July. Life is good here in Savannah she thinks to herself. Pete enjoys his job, his family is here, my sister, Willene, lives nearby, and now, this news. She was looking forward to babysitting!

With the long hours Pete was putting in, that meant a larger paycheck. They had just purchased their first car, a 1931 Model A. That was all they could afford at the present time, but were hoping for something a little newer in the very near future. It is now April - spring and warmer temperatures. Yes! she says to herself. This is her favorite time of the year. Since they now own a car, she can take Pete to work. She didn't mind getting up and taking him to work. She was thankful for the car that could get her to the grocery store, the laundromat, and to the library.

"Pete," Quinelle calls out to him as he is dressing for work, "do you think we could possibly attend Aunt Daisy's birthday dinner in June, since we have a car now?"

"I don't see why we can't do that."

"Maybe Charles and Willene will go with us. That would be fun!" Quinelle continued, "And maybe we could go up on Saturday and visit with your brother, Nathaniel and Etheel? I can get her to trim my hair while I'm there. Can't believe they have two little boys now. Larry was just six months old when we got married, and another boy this year, what's his name? Oh, yea...Tarrell. We could stay overnight at their house; Willene and Charles could stay with Aunt Daisy, I'm sure. I would get to see Pearlene and Georgia. I have really missed them...."

"Whoa, slow down," Pete says as he whirls around for a kiss, "You are really excited about this, aren't you?

"As much as I love you and love our life together, I really miss everyone in Uvalda. It will be 10 months in June since I have seen them, especially Pearlene and Georgia, and my best friend, Etta Mae. She has been married to Carl for a couple of months now. It will be fun to visit her and Carl in their new home in Uvalda. Just think, we will be in the "old" married couples Sunday School class when we go to church that Sunday."

"Write your letters and put Nathaniel and Etheel on notice that we are planning on coming on that Saturday before the birthday dinner. I'll ask for that Saturday off. I'm sure it won't be a problem. Things are slowing down a bit at work. As a matter of fact, Bro. Poole told us yesterday that we wouldn't be putting in as many hours beginning next week." Pete informed her.

"Oh, is everything okay?" Quinelle looked a little worried.

"I think so. Don't worry. Everything will work out. God takes care of us, remember?"

"Yes, I know. We better get going," she said as she grabbed her pocketbook and Pete's lunch she had prepared.

"What are your plans for the day?" Pete asked as they were headed to the construction site.

"I'm going to the Five and Dime to buy some material to make me a new dress for the birthday dinner," she announced happily.

Pete just shook his head and laughed. "Okay, I go to work, you spend it."

"Oh, Pete, you know I haven't....."

"Just kidding, go have fun! I love you".

They kissed quickly as he leaned over to the driver's side.

"Love you, too".

As she drove off, she could only think of how much she was in love with Pete Stokes, and what a bright future they had. She could just feel it. Thank you, God, for the sunshine after the rain. Just then, she looked up in the sky, and saw the most beautiful rainbow.

Chapter 20

Oh, good. Sunshine today. *The picture window* was framing the beautiful sights of spring. Was it last night that Pete told me that my sisters were coming today? I hope it is today. I haven't seen Willene and Pearlene since Thanksgiving. Our families usually get together here at our house in Haynesville. My oldest sister, Lois and her husband, Wes, didn't make it up from Florida this past Thanksgiving,

The phone rang. I can hear Pete's voice from the kitchen as he answers it.

"Good morning, sweetheart", Pete said as he leaned over and pecked me on my cheek and held my hand, "That was Willene on the phone. She will be leaving Atlanta in about forty-five minutes, so that means she should be here in about three hours. Pearlene and Lois are just now leaving Savannah, so they should all arrive about the same time."

"I was hoping I had remembered right, that today is the day for their visit."

"As soon as you eat a little something, Etheel should be here to wash and roll your hair. That will make you feel a lot better, I know," Pete told me as he caressed my hair.

"Okay," I said, "help me to sit up. This is going to be a great day!"

I could hear MaMa puttering around in the kitchen. She was preparing some toast for my breakfast. That's about all I can keep down - dry toast, no butter.

Pete left to finish getting ready for the day as MaMa brought in my toast and juice.

"I bet you are looking forward to seeing all your sisters again," MaMa said as she put my breakfast on my tray.

"It has been a while since the four of us have been together. I hope I can stay awake for their visit. I told Pete I didn't want any pain medication this morning; that makes me really drowsy."

"Well, eat up. Etheel will be here in a few minutes to do your hair. I'm going to do a little straightening up around the house before your sisters get here."

"Thanks, MaMa."

Etheel helps me to the chair she has arranged in front of the downstairs guest bathroom sink where she washes my hair. I am too weak to get in the shower nowadays. While there, she gives me a sponge bath.

"I'm looking forward to seeing Willene and Pearlene again. Some 'good ole' memories!" Etheel reflected. "It's hard to believe that J.N. and I ended up living in the same neighborhood in Warner Robins as Willene and Charles many years ago."

"I know, and the good fortune that Charles got transferred to Robins Air Force Base, of all places. After they were in England for three years and I hadn't seen my sister all that time; what a wonderful surprise that was. God knew I needed my sister close by." I smiled just thinking about those happy times when our children were growing up and getting to spend a lot of time together as cousins; sort of like when I was growing up with my cousins.

Etheel helped me to the living room chair where I usually sat under the hair dryer for about an hour for it to get dry. This routine of Etheel washing, rolling, and fixing my hair had taken the place of my regular beauty shop appointment each week over in Warner Robins. I had used the same hairdresser for over 10 years. I miss that, but am so thankful for Etheel.

While I was getting my hair dry, Etheel said she was going

fishing, and would be back to fix my hair. Etheel and I both dearly love to fish!

'Pete's Paradise' has several ponds that we fish. When David, (Pete's Dad) was alive, the ponds were open to the public, and Granddaddy, as he was affectionately called, would collect the money. He also sold bait and tackle from a little shed on the property. He would ride the property on his golf cart.

I miss my fishing! I've always enjoyed fishing, even when I was a small child. Everyone said I got that from my Daddy. He would rather be fishing than anything, I was told. The last time I spent any time with my Dad was fishing in these ponds. I had invited him to come visit. We had not seen each other in quite some time. His health was deteriorating; I thought coming here and fishing these ponds would do him some good. It was a time of healing for me, also.

I impatiently look at my watch. I turn off the dryer, take out my curlers. (I can still do that!). Hope Etheel doesn't lose track of time. I need to get dressed, too. Pete had laid out my clothes on the sofa, but I usually need help these days to even get dressed. I don't like being so dependent on my family! Lord, why is this happening to me?

I want to look my best for my sisters. I don't want to them to feel sorry for me, but I know what they were thinking when they made plans to come together and visit. This may be the last time we see each other until we get to heaven. I'm not going to cry....I will be strong. Lord Jesus, help me today to be strong for my sisters. Thank you for this time we do get to spend together. I was praying silently when Etheel walked in.

"I'm back," Etheel sang out as she entered the back door. "As soon as I wash my hands, I'll fix your hair and help you get dressed. I caught supper for tonight! Three large bass."

I waited until Etheel came into the room before I responded, "Which pond did you catch them in?"

"The one right here behind the house, standing right there on the little bridge."

"I'm jealous."

"I'll tell Pete there will be enough for he and MaMa for their supper, too." Etheel offered.

"They will like that!"

Etheel teased and fixed my hair and helped me get dressed. She brought my make-up from the bathroom, and I proceeded to apply a little foundation, a little eyeliner, a little mascara, and a little lipstick. I had finally gotten away from the 'bondage' of the old church teachings against make-up. I realized God was really more concerned about what's on the inside that the outside. But, I am very conservative in the use of make-up. My thinking is God doesn't want Christian women to look like tramps, either.

The visit with my sisters was wonderful. Lois had driven up from Florida to Savannah and rode up with Pearlene. They had called Ann, who is living in Vidalia, to ask if she wanted to come, too. They would pick her up on the way. Ann is my brother, Morris', daughter. Both Morris and her Mother, Annette, are deceased. Ann is a single mom with a grown son now. Her son, Bill, spent the last couple of summers hanging out with us. Pete and I have helped Ann out over the years with some of her expenses. She has always struggled. She always had a job, but it was still hard to make ends meet. Anyway, Pearlene said Ann was too sick to come. She really wanted to come, but knew it wouldn't be good for her to be around me. Needless to say, I was sorely disappointed.

They all arrived around 10:00. Pete went into town and picked up some Skipper John's chicken and all the fixins' for lunch. He, MaMa, and Etheel joined us for a leisurely lunch out on the deck, then disappeared so I could have some time alone with my sisters.

I haven't laughed this much in a while. We reminisced

about so many things. How good it is to watch my sisters en-joying themselves!

I am getting tired, but I don't want it to show. Pearlene an-nounces around 4:00 that they need to get on the road. She wants to be back home in Savannah before it gets too late. Willene acknowledges that she needs to get back, also. We all stand to say our good-byes.

Here come the tears. I can't hold them back. Just the thought that I may never see my sisters again......

There's so much I want to say, and the same with them, I can tell; but the words don't come.

As they leave to get into their cars, Pete helps me back to the bed. I watch my sisters, and wave good-bye to them from *the picture window.*

Chapter 21

Quinelle and Pete arrive back home in Savannah after a full weekend of visiting in Uvalda, and ending with the birthday dinner at the community house. Pearlene and Georgia rode back with them for a two week visit - one week at Willene's house, and one week at Quinelle's. The girls were out on summer vacation. They had only one more year of high school before graduating.

Savannah was a great place to be for the annual Fourth of July celebration. Pete, Quinelle, Willene, Charles and the girls attended the parade. Uvalda didn't have parades or fireworks! They walked the town squares with their splurge of ice cream and sodas. They all joined up later at Lamar and Martha's house along with Pete's Mother, his Daddy and Coot for a cookout. Lamar and his three daughters, Jessi, Linda, and Elaine were able to watch the parade from their house. Martha was 'too pregnant' to take the heat and all that standing. Her baby was due in a couple of weeks. After the cookout, they waited in anticipation of the fireworks. Only Lamar's family had seen fireworks before!

After the fireworks, Lamar's girls were off to play again. Willene and Charles left to go home. Willene was just about a couple of months away from the birth of their baby, and was feeling very tired. Coot was now 17; Pearlene and Georgia both 16 years of age. The girls had known him from the church in Uvalda, and in elementary and junior high school, so they were not strangers to one another. They played board games while the adults relaxed and talked.

After talking about the events of the day while still seated around the dining table, Pete's Dad, David said, "Your Momma and I have made a decision. You know work has slowed down quite a bit. My conversation with Brother Poole a couple of weeks ago was not very good. He doesn't think there will be enough work for all of us in the next few months, and that he will probably have to lay us off."

"Did Bro. Poole say anything to you, Pete, about this?" asked Quinelle.

"Well, yes...." Pete answered with hesitation.

Quinelle looked from Pete to David.

"So what is this decision you've made?" Lamar asked of his Dad.

"Lucille and I received a letter from your sister, Betty, a few days ago. You know they live near Robins Air Force Base in Warner Robins, Ga. Her husband, Robert, is saying that the residential building going on there is picking up at a really fast pace - mainly because of the Air Force Base and new folks being stationed there. Robert thought we might be interested since he knew things were slowing down here for us. Your Momma could be there to help with Betty's two children; Calvin, who was just born, as you know, back in February, and Diane, who is now three years old. They have told us we could live with them until we were able to get a place of our own."

"What about Coot? What does he think about it?" asked Pete.

Upon hearing his name, Coot joined the conversation, "I've decided to join the Air Force. I'll be eighteen soon. But, I'm moving to Warner Robins with Momma and Daddy for now."

Pete asked his Dad, "When are you planning on making this move?"

David answered, "Since our lease is up at the end of next

month, we will move out sometime before the end of August."
Lucille nodded.

"What will you do, Pete, if Bro. Poole has to let you go?"
Coot questioned his brother.

"I'm not sure. I haven't had a chance to discuss this with
Quinelle yet," Pete looked guiltily at his wife. He had not
wanted to worry her.

He had thought he would wait to tell her after Pearlene
and Georgia returned home. But, the subject had been
broached before he could tell her.

Lamar interjected, "You could always come back to work
for Bankers, I'm sure."

"Or, ya'll could move to Warner Robins, too," Coot
chimed in.

"Why not think about it, Pete?" David continued, "We can
go on ahead and look for work there, and then you and
Quinelle could come later. We will be looking around, also, for
a place to live. Ya'll could stay with us until you find yourselves
a place."

"I don't know......," Pete said when he got that 'look' from
Quinelle that it was time to go.

Martha pushed her chair back from the table. "I need to
check on the girls. Time for baths and bedtime."

Quinelle stood up also and said, "Send them in here for
a minute so we can say our good-byes. It's time we headed
home."

"We need to go, too," MaMa echoed, "Tell those girls
MaMa needs some good-night sugar."

As the three granddaughters were giving hugs and kisses,
David laughingly said to Lamar, "How do you like being surrounded by all these females?"

"Gets a little crazy around here, sometimes, but I'm okay
with it. I am hoping the next one will be a Junior."

They all laughed and exchanged 'good nights' to one
another as they exited to their individual homes.

Quinelle was silent on the way home. She was thinking about what Pete would do if he got fired or laid off from his job. What would they do?

The possibility that he might have to go back to work with Bankers was not a pleasant thought because she knew he did not enjoy that job. On the other hand, the thought of leaving Savannah and Willene was more than she could bear.

She looked out the car window. She really liked Savannah and their life here. She was happy here. She would be strong, and hold back the tears that were on the verge of being released. Lord, help to guide Pete in his decisions, and I will try my best to do whatever it is I need to do to make it easier for him.

Chapter 22

Pete and Quinelle stopped by Charles and Willene's on their way home from the job site. They were anxious to meet their new niece that has just been born a couple of days ago.

"Well...... what did you finally decide to name her?" Quinelle asked as she held out her arms to take the newborn.

"Carolyn is her name," Charles announced proudly.

"Hello, Carolyn," as she bent her head down to kiss the baby, "I'm Aunt Quinelle or Aunt Nell, which ever you prefer." Willene still called her Nell. "You are so tiny and beautiful."

"Nell, let's take Carolyn into the bedroom. I think she needs changing."

As the ladies left for the bedroom, Pete and Charles sat down on the couch and talked about the hot weather, and how rain was badly needed, and such things as men talk about.

Quinelle sat down on the bed while Willene changed the baby's diaper. "I'm so happy for you, Willene, and glad things went well with the delivery."

Willene was talking gibberish to the baby as Quinelle stood up and said, "Willene, I think I might be pregnant. I missed my period this month."

"We need to get you a doctor's appointment. You could go to my doctor and he will confirm whether you are or not. You could wait until you miss a second period before going."

"I want to have a baby, but the timing is not good," Quinelle looked downcast.

"What do you mean? Pete's job?

"Yea, Brother Poole told him that he would only need him two or three days next week, and after that, he wasn't sure what was going to happen."

"What are ya'll going to do?" Willene was worried now.

"We're not sure, but as much as I hate the thought of this, we may be moving to Warner Robins."

Willene hugged Quinelle tightly and said, "You can't leave me. Who am I going to use for a babysitter?" Willene tried to laugh, but was not doing a good job at hiding her disappointment.

"We are praying about this, Willene," Quinelle said trying to regain her composure. She didn't want to cry right now. So many emotions! She's happy for Willene; she's happy at the thought that she might be pregnant, but distressed at the same time!

"I'm feeling pretty tired, Nell. I need to lie down while Carolyn is sleeping." Willene laid the baby in the crib near the bed. "Let me know if you decide to make a doctor's appointment. Have you told Pete yet?"

"Oh, no. I wanted to be pretty sure before I said anything."

"Just keep me posted," Willene said as she prepared to lie down. "And, thanks for the vegetable soup and cornbread you made for us. Charles loves homemade vegetable soup."

"You're welcome. I'll come by tomorrow again to check on you. Love you." Quinelle pulled the drapes in the bedroom and shut the door on her way out.

Chapter 23

The fateful day was approaching fast. They were moving to Warner Robins. Lucille and Coot had decided to stay in Savannah while David went on to Warner Robins to look for work. He had met a builder there by the name of Doc Cameron, who was in need of sheetrock hangers and flooring contractors. David stayed with Betty and Robert a couple of months until he had found a small home to rent. Now, it was time to bring Lucille and Coot to Warner Robins. Pete and Quinelle had decided to hitch a ride with Pete's Momma and Dad to Warner Robins. They had sold their car. It wasn't worth much; and didn't think it would make the trip, anyway! Moving day was scheduled for the Friday after Thanksgiving. They had just celebrated Thanksgiving with Lamar and his family. David drove down from Warner Robins; Willene, Charles, and Carolyn came over, too. This would be their last celebration all together. Quinelle was having a hard time feeling thankful.

Brother Poole had to let Pete go; just not enough work. He had kept Pete on the payroll as long as he could. David had called Lamar and told him to tell Pete that Doc Cameron could use another hired hand, and for Pete to start working as soon as he got here.

"I'm going to miss this place," Quinelle said as she packed up her sewing machine and accessories.

"This place? You must be joking!" Pete looked at her with a puzzled look on his face.

"Well, I won't miss sharing a bathroom with two other couples, that's for sure", with a chuckle, "but this little apartment will always have a special place in my heart. Our first place," Quinelle spoke dreamily as she paused in her packing.

Pete walked over and gave her a big bear hug. She started crying - again! "I don't mean to cry so much. I'm sorry, Pete."

"I know this is hard for you, but I believe this is the right thing to do." Pete reassured her. "I'm sure you being pregnant makes you a little more emotional, so your sister told me."

"Probably so, and this morning sickness I have been having isn't helping!" She backed out of his arms. "I need to get back to this packing."

"Don't wear yourself out. Take a break when you are feeling tired. One good thing - we don't have that much to pack up!" Pete trying to cheer Quinelle up.

"I'm so glad Willene, Charles and the baby made it over to Lamar's yesterday for Thanksgiving. That Carolyn is growing so fast! What if we have a girl? What would we name her? I like Suzette." Quinelle's sad demeanor seem to almost vanish with talk of the baby.

"We have 8 months to think about baby names."

"I sure hope we can have our own place before the baby comes. Do you think that is possible?"

"Anything is possible, Quinelle. Let's trust God for that, okay?"

"Okay, and I promise I will be patient. I do love you, Pete Stokes."

"I love you, too, Quinelle Stokes."

Pete walked back to the couch. He needed to study the Sunday School lesson he was scheduled to teach tomorrow. This was to be their last Sunday in the small Pentecostal church he had grown to love. His class consisted of a few fourth and fifth graders. He thoroughly enjoyed teaching each Sunday.

He glanced over at Quinelle working away in the kitchen. She was so beautiful to him, inside and out. She meant so much to him. He knew that he could never live without her. She was his strength.

Yes, she cried when he told her that the move to Warner Robins was what they needed to do. But, she cried, too, when she told him she was pregnant. She cries when she is sad, and cries when she is happy. She is a strong little lady, and does her best whatever the situation. Her strength made him stronger. She made him smile.

She glanced over at Pete studying his lesson. Such a handsome man! A good, hard-working, Christian man. She trusted him with her life. Everything was going to be okay. She just knew it!

Chapter 24

Through *the picture window I* can see the pine trees swaying in the gentle breeze. I can even *feel* the breeze. I raise myself up, and see that the windows in the room have been opened. That's why I can feel the wind! It's the first day of May and I'm still alive! I'm not sure if that's a good thing or not. I'm still believing God for my healing. But, I feel my time here on earth is drawing to a close - soon now. And, I'm not sure if that's such a bad thing. Some days, I want to go on to heaven. I know Pete and the children don't want me to leave them.

"Honey, the grandchildren want to come in and see you. Is that okay with you?" Pete asks me.

"I guess so. I do want to see them, I just don't like them to see me like this."

"I won't let them stay long. But, they really miss you and ask about you all the time."

They come into the room and gather around my bed. They are so very quiet. They just look at me, and don't say a word.

"How's school going, kids? I bet ya'll are glad school will soon be out for summer." I tried to sound as 'normal' as I could.

"I'm ready for school to be out," Neilie, my oldest granddaughter, blurted out.

"Me, too," said Shane and Heather simultaneously. Luke was not yet old enough to go to school. Danna is only two years old. She would always stand on a stool next to my bed. Many times she would stand there and pray for me.

There was a wall of silence. I could tell the kids were uncomfortable around me, and didn't know what to say.

I proceeded to ask each one of them something about their subjects in school and ask if they were behaving in school. I asked Luke what he had been doing all day. He said something about his Momma teaching him a new game called Crazy Eights.

Pete was standing in the room along with my children and their spouses, just watching from a distance. I think he could tell I was exhausted. I didn't want them to go, but keeping up the conversation was not an easy task.

Pete approached the children, "Mema is tired. She needs her rest now. Ya'll go on out and fish, how about it?"

Each one of the grandchildren hugged me and told me that they loved me. Not sure how I came to be called Mema, but the oldest grandchild, Neilie, was the instigator!

"I love you all so much. Be good! Oh, catch a bunch of fish for me!" I try to sound chipper as my voice wavers.

The grandchildren went outside to fish, except Danna, while my children stayed and visited with me for a few minutes. The chatter was making me agitated. It was good to see them, but I was trying my best not to nod off. Their voices were fading in and out. I was trying my best to keep up. Chris, my only son, was sitting on the edge of the bed, holding my hand. Standing on both sides of me were Connie and Gwen, my daughters. This isn't real. I can't believe this is happening to me. I can feel their love. I also feel like I'm suffocating. Please everyone, just leave me alone.

I look around the room. Everyone is gone. I guess I dozed off. The lights are dim, and the curtains have been drawn across *the picture window*. I hope I see sunshine tomorrow.

Left – Daisy Clark – Quinelle's Aunt
Right – Pearl Yeomans – Quinelle's Mother

Bottom (l-r) Pearlene,Quinelle
Top (l-r) Willene, Morris

Willene

Quinelle & Pete – circa 1951

Quinelle & Pete

Stokes Bros. Construction Work Truck

Lamar's Insurance Agency &
Stokes Bros. Const. offices

Quinelle and Pete – circa 1960

(l-r) – Willene, Quinelle, Pearlene,
Lemmie (their Dad), Lois

Quinelle – circa 1964

Chapter 25

David's car is loaded with our few earthly possessions. He, David, had made an earlier trip prior to Thanksgiving and moved the majority of their belongings. Our apartment had been furnished, so we had no furniture to move. Everything we owned was packed away in two suitcases and three large cardboard boxes, with the exception of my sewing machine. Lamar and his family will be coming up to visit us at Christmas time, and will bring the few boxes that belonged to his Mom and Dad that wouldn't fit into the car this trip. Lamar's station wagon came in handy!

We watched the sunrise over Savannah for the last time before heading on our journey to Warner Robins. Pete will start his new job with Mr. Cameron on Monday morning. No time to waste. Off we go onto a new adventure. At least the morning sickness had subsided the last couple of days. And, it's a beautiful day for traveling. We had everything on the sidewalk awaiting our ride to Warner Robins.

"It was a sad Wednesday night at church saying good-bye to our friends. I grew to love that little church," Quinelle said longingly. "Hope that church that your Momma and Daddy are attending is just as friendly."

"According to Momma, they are really enjoying the preachin'," Pete replied.

"I just hope he teaches about the love of God and not

always about hell." Quinelle said as she turned to look up at their abandoned apartment.

Just as Quinelle was thinking about going back into the apartment for warmth, she saw their ride rounding the corner. "Thank goodness! It's so cold out here!" She grabbed up a suitcase to load it into the trunk. Pete grabbed it from her and reminded her that she is expecting, and to just get in the car.

She climbed into the back seat, not really wanting to leave Savannah and her sister. "Help me, Lord," as she took a deep breath, and let it out slowly.

There were a lot of mixed emotions being felt by everyone in the car. Lucille was thinking of her grandchildren she was leaving behind; Coot was already missing his newfound friends; Quinelle distraught over leaving her sister again; and Pete hoping he was in God's will in making this move.

Leaving the outskirts of Savannah, Lucille turns to Quinelle in the back seat. "Are you warm enough back there, Quinelle?"

"Yes, I'm fine."

"Now, if you feel sick, just tell David to pull over, okay?"

"I will, but I have been feeling better the last couple of days."

"Have you thought of names yet for the baby?" Lucille continued.

"Not really," Pete replied, "We've got plenty of time for that."

"How about Lucille?" Everyone laughed at Lucille's suggestion.

Quinelle curled up next to Pete and yawned. They had gotten up quite early, and she was more tired than usual these days.

Coot was already leaning his head against the window pane in the front seat, with his Momma seated between his Daddy and himself. He was in a very somber mood, and didn't have much to say. David never had much to say anyway, anytime. So, it seemed no one in the vehicle was wanting to talk much. Everyone was exhausted from the physical and emotional drain of this move.

Quinelle was already missing Charles, Willene, and the baby. She had coddled Carolyn practically the entire time of their Thanksgiving visit. Willene had promised that they would come visit once she learned that they had moved into a place of their own. She didn't want to intrude on David and Lucille while Pete and Quinelle were living there. But, be assured she would come, and bring Pearlene with her, no matter where they lived, when the baby was born.

About an hour and a half into the trip, David pulls into a small country store. Everyone is aroused from their napping.

"Break time!" David announces.

"Good!" Quinelle exclaimed softly to Pete, "my bladder is full!" She makes a dash for the restroom.

As the family stretches while in the store drinking their RC Colas and eating Moonpies, moods seem to brighten up. Pete and Coot were ribbing one another as was the usual. The Stokes family had always had lots of laughter in their home. It always seemed no matter what the circumstances, the problems, or sometimes not knowing where the money was coming from to pay the bills, the Stokes family never lost their sense of humor! Quinelle was glad to be a part of this fun-loving family. The future didn't seem so bleak after all.

Chapter 26

Work was plentiful. Pete, Coot and their Dad worked steadily during the holiday season, right up until Christmas Day. Lamar and his family drove up to spend Christmas with everyone. Christmas dinner was held at Betty and Robert's home. Nathaniel and Etheel and their two boys, also, joined them. A great homecoming! Everyone together again!

Willene and Charles were spending Christmas at Charles' Mom and Dad's in Vidalia. Pearlene was spending the Christmas holidays with Willene and Charles, so she was in Vidalia, too. This was Quinelle's first Christmas without her sisters. She didn't have time to be sad, though, with all these Stokes' around! She enjoyed playing with all the children. Lamar now had four children; Nathaniel had two, and Betty, their sister, had two. What a lively bunch! The weather was unseasonably warm for December, so the children could run and play outside - that was a good thing. Lots of cooking and chattering was going on in Betty's kitchen. The men folk gathered together, talking of work and the economy.

"When are you moving out?" Lamar asked Pete, after learning that Pete had found a house to rent.

"Plans are to move the first of February. This house is owned by Roger Davis, who is the mayor of Warner Robins. Mr. Davis lives next door to Momma and Daddy's house; and when he learned we were in the construction business; he told me if I would do some repairs and fix up a house he owns on

Third Street, that Quinelle and I could move into it. I should be through with the work needed by the end of next month." Pete went on excitedly, "That sure makes Quinelle happy. It's small, but it will be our own place."

"Yea, it's difficult living in a house with two women!" Nathaniel proclaimed with a grin.

"I heard that!" Lucille retorted. As the norm, the whole Stokes clan began to laugh and continued their bantering about the subject of womenfolk.

"You know the old sayin', if Momma ain't happy, ain't nobody happy!" David entered the conversation after just sitting back, watching and enjoying the laughter of his adult children.

"Okay, you guys, go wash up, call the children in, time to eat," ordered Martha from the dining table. "The children will eat here at the kitchen table; adults in the dining room."

As everyone gathers together around the dining room table, each grabs a hand of the one standing next to him. Everyone bows their heads as Lamar commences to say the blessing over the food. Never is a meal eaten without a blessing being said over it! This prayer today is more than just asking a blessing over our food, but to remember the reason for our celebrating today. Today is the birthday of our Lord and King Jesus Christ. Lamar gives thanks to God for the many ways He has taken care of this family.

As the blessing is being offered up, Quinelle thinks back to earlier times and Christmases in Uvalda with her Aunt Daisy and Uncle Otis, and all her cousins. This was the way she was raised. She was thankful that she had married Pete, and they and his family were carrying out the same traditions. She really missed her "family", but this family was a wonderful family to be a part of. She was thinking of the many cousins their baby would have in its' life; just as she had growing up. Once again, she thanks God for the blessing of being a part of this family, and one filled with such love for one another.

Chapter 27

Moving day arrived finally. It didn't take long, seeing how there was not much to move! Pete and Quinelle had purchased a bed, a couch, a chair, and a dining table with two chairs for their new abode. Pete was currently working on Barker's Furniture Store in Warner Robins, helping to put a new roof on the building. The owner, Mr. C.W. Barker, worked it out with Pete on the furniture, allowing Pete to make small monthly payments. The house was very small, but, it was a house just for the two of them and the new baby on the way. Quinelle had written Willene and Pearlene in hopes they could come for a visit soon, even before the baby is due.

Pearlene wrote back reminding her that she wouldn't be able to come visit until school was out. This was her senior year and she didn't want to miss out on anything. Hopefully, she could come visit when the baby was born in July. Willene also wrote of the hardship it would be traveling alone with Carolyn right now. Charles was working so much that this was not a good time for him, either.

Nineteen years old, a baby on the way, married to the man she loves, and now, a home of their own! Work had been plentiful. She and Pete prayed nightly, and thanked God for their good fortune. Not that they had a lot, but God had provided for their needs. Every paycheck Pete received, they made sure to give God his ten percent. They believed and trusted God to honor them in their tithing. It was hard to do at times, but they knew giving back to God was the right thing to do. Life was good - so far!

Quinelle was enjoying her role as the happy homemaker in her new home. She made curtains and a tablecloth for the new dining table. She would have to wait on curtains for the baby's room until the baby arrived. Until then, she wouldn't know the gender of the baby.

Now, it's been two months since the move into their new home. Lucille has come to visit, bringing with her a letter. Their houses were only two blocks from each other. The beautiful spring weather permitted Lucille to walk the short distance.

Lucille found Quinelle tending to the small yard. Some flowers had been planted previously in the yard, and were just blooming with the warm spring air.

"Pretty flowers, aren't they?" Lucille commented.

"Yes, they are. I was so glad to see them bloom a couple of days ago."

"This letter from the Draft Board came this morning for Pete," Lucille said as she handed the letter to Quinelle.

Quinelle took the envelope from Lucille, with fear in her eyes. Oh, no, she thought, this can't be. "Thanks, Lucille, I'll give it to Pete as soon as he comes in from work."

Lucille followed her inside to the small kitchen, where Quinelle laid the letter on the table. "How about some water to drink?" Quinelle offering Lucille a glass of tap water.

"Yes, that would be good." Lucille knew it would be best if she didn't talk about the letter.

"You've got this place looking real cozy, Quinelle, you have a knack for decorating."

"Thank you. We are really happy here - not that we weren't happy at your place..."

"I know what you mean, Quinelle," as Lucille chuckled, "it's good that you and Pete have your own place."

After a few minutes of chit-chat, Lucille started back home, stating she had to get dinner started.

Quinelle waved good-bye to Lucille from the back door, then turned to go to the kitchen to start her own dinner. The letter on the table stared her in the face. Oh, God, she prayed, not now. The baby will be here in three months.

Chapter 28

Oh, the pain! I feel as though I'm giving birth!

I suddenly realize I've been dreaming again. But the "dreams" are not really dreams – my mind is taking me back to earlier events in my life. The medication for my pain is to blame, I'm sure.

The medication has apparently worn off as the pain is real. The pain in my abdomen is from the hysterectomy that was performed during my surgery. The exploratory surgery confirmed that cancer had spread into my stomach. The removal of my female organs was to keep the cancer from spreading to those organs as well. This second bout with cancer, after surviving almost five years from breast cancer, was discovered just a few months ago. The doctors sewed me up and gave me little hope of surviving more than six months. This is the fourth month.

"Quinelle, I'm here."

My dear and faithful husband as always. He very rarely leaves this room anymore. He has put his construction business on hold for now. There seems to always be someone here when I awake. It's mostly the pain that awakens me now. It must be dark; the curtains on *the picture window* are drawn; my view of the outside world is closed to me. I don't like the night time anymore. I'm so afraid I won't wake up to see another sunrise or another day... period.

I hear Pete stirring out of his recliner where he has been

resting. The television is rarely turned on so as not to disturb me. Pete has given up quite a few things for me. I don't want him waiting on me; I want to wait on him! That's the way it has been and that's the way it should be. He has been such a good provider. A wonderful husband and father.

"Are you in a lot of pain, Quinelle?" Pete asks as he places his hand on my forehead, brushing back the hair from my face.

"I was dreaming again....remembering the pain of child-birth as I was giving birth to Connie. It was so real. But, I guess I was *really* in pain and that is why I awoke."

"Do you want me to give you some morphine?"

"Not yet, Pete. It makes me so drowsy, and I want to talk to you for a while before the shot."

"Okay, but let me get you some watermelon juice I have prepared. You seem to be able to keep that down better than anything else so far."

"Sounds good. The pain is not quite so intense at the moment."

As Pete brings the juice to me, I'm thinking back to where I left off before I awoke. I had just given birth to Connie, our firstborn. That was July 1952.

"So, what do you want to talk about?" Pete inquires as he helps her with the glass of juice.

"Help me sit up and you sit here beside me." She pats the area on the bed next to her.

"I was just thinking about the draft notice you received a few months before Connie was born....."

"Yea, I remember that day very well. We were both so nervous about opening that letter."

"I thought I was going to faint when I saw you were classi-fied 1A and was told to report in 30 days."

"Well, I took care of that, didn't I?" Pete was laughing.

"Your sure did. What was it? Just two weeks before you were to report, you broke your leg?"

"I think so. Looking back, sometimes bad things that happen to us, happen for a reason. Because of that broken leg, I was exempted."

"I was so thankful...not for your broken leg, but that you didn't have to leave me."

"Be thankful to God. I truly believe He was looking after us. Mr. C.W. and Bertha Barker were especially kind to us, since it was the roof of their furniture store I was working on when I fell."

Pete stood up and offered me more juice. It seemed to be helping somewhat. At least, I wasn't feeling nauseous right now.

"Pete, remember the ride to Macon to get to the hospital? I was sitting in the middle between you and Pearlene in the red pick-up truck you had just bought, holding on for dear life speeding over all those railroad tracks!"

"I was terrified you were going to have that baby before I could get you to the hospital. It would have been nice if Warner Robins had had a hospital back then."

The two of us were laughing. It felt good to laugh!

"I was so glad Pearlene came to stay with us. She was a great help with Connie, and taking care of me and the house."

"I remember like it was yesterday how excited you were to see her. It had been about a year since the two of you had been together."

"Pete, the watermelon juice is kicking in. I need you to get me to the bathroom."

As was the usual, he bent down so I could wrap my arms around his neck. It felt good to feel my arms around him. He lifted me up and carried me as if I was nothing. Not sure how much I weigh now, but I know I have lost quite a bit of weight.

Now back in bed, Pete gives me a shot of morphine for the now intense pain I am feeling once again.

"Good night, sweetheart."

"Good night, Pete, I love you."

"I love you, too, Quinelle, and I *will* see you in the morning."

I'm feeling quite drowsy. I am fighting it because I don't want to go back to sleep just yet. That's all I do anymore! If I go to sleep, I may not wake up. I don't mind waking up if tomorrow I'm healed of this cancer. I know Jesus can heal me, but will He?

I turn away from *the picture window*. I don't want to see the curtains drawn. I'm tired of looking at those green curtains. My "curtain" of life is being closed too soon. I'm so lonely, Lord Jesus.

I can feel a presence in the room. I call out. No one answers me. A peacefulness engulfs me. I drift off into oblivion.... again.

Chapter 29

Willene and Carolyn's visit was way too short! They had come up from Savannah for the weekend to meet Constance, their new niece and cousin, respectively. Willene was taking Pearlene back home with her to live. Pearlene had graduated from high school back in May, and wanted to live with Willene and Charles in Savannah. The plan was for Pearlene to find a job as soon as possible. Having a built-in babysitter would surely be a plus for Willene!

"You and Pete come for a weekend soon," Willene begged as they prepared to leave.

"We will."

"I still can't believe how things have changed for you both. Pete breaking his leg changed everything."

"It sure did!" reiterated Quinelle, "Life has been interesting, that's for sure. God has been so good to us."

Pearlene added, "And moving into a new house, too!"

"Let's go, Pearlene," as Willene picked up Carolyn and placed her in the car. "Savannah, here we come."

"Be careful. Love you all," as Quinelle waved to her sisters and niece. "Had fun!"

Quinelle decided to water her flower garden before going back into the house. The baby was asleep, as was Pete, taking *his* regular Sunday afternoon nap. She would take this opportunity while she had it! Taking care of a baby was indeed a full-time job. Being an Aunt to several children had already prepared her in some ways to be a Mother. Just a little different, though!

While Pete was recovering from his broken leg, he, of course, was not able to work. That was really hard on him. David and Coot were spending a lot of their time over in Macon where the building business was in full swing also due in part to the Air Force Base in Warner Robins. They took care of Pete, as families do, while he was recuperating.

Pondering all these events made Quinelle smile as she finished watering the flowers. Life was good......

"Hey, sweetheart, the baby is awake and I think she's hungry," Pete announced as he walked toward her.

"Well, I guess I better get inside seeing as how I'm the only one that can take care of that!" She laughed as she playfully threw a soft blow to his abdomen. In reaction, he grabbed her arm and pulled her body into his arms, and landed a kiss on her forehead.

They went into the house with their arms wrapped around each other.

"Hard to believe we will all be moving – again – in just a few weeks."

"Yea, we will be in the same neighborhood as Momma and Daddy. Their new home we are building for them should be completed in just a couple of weeks. I am so happy for them."

"Yes, isn't that wonderful? I am so excited and so thankful for our new home-to-be. Constance will have a room of her own. I hope I will have the curtains completed before time to move."

"I'm sure you will, if I know you! And, boy, do I know you!!" He gave her a wink and a peck on her cheek.

"Go away, Pete Stokes, I'm trying to feed the baby."

Chapter 30

There was no warning! Who knew or would have ever thought a tornado would hit Warner Robins, Georgia? But, it happened on April 30, 1953. The Air Force Base was the hardest hit and a few areas off the base. Some apartments called Ziegler Apartments were totally destroyed. They were located close to our offices. Thank goodness, there was only one fatality. Our offices were not affected; just a lot of debris in the streets.

David and Coot were in Macon working on a construction site; Pete was working in Warner Robins; the rest of us were in our respective homes. As you can imagine there was much panic in the town. By now we had telephones in our homes and were able to call out to check on everyone. We all breathed a sigh of relief and thankfulness to God.

We have been in our new home for a few months now and are expecting our second child in September. Pete is certainly hoping for a boy this time. How am I going to handle two children – just fourteen months apart?

Willene and Etheel are both expecting, too! I wish they were here. Pete and I are planning a weekend trip to Savannah soon.

It will probably be sometime in June. I can hardly wait to see that sweet little niece, Carolyn. She and Constance will get a chance to get acquainted this time. We will also get to visit with Lamar and Martha and their children. It's great to have cousins!

18 months later

"Can you believe it? My sister, Betty and Robert are going to open a fish market and restaurant right near our offices?" Pete revealed to Quinelle.

"Are you serious?"

"Yes, he came by the office today and told me it was going to happen and soon."

"Is Betty going to work there? How about the children?"

"I didn't ask all that, Quinelle."

"Why not? I would have."

"I'm sure they have figured all that out. Maybe Momma is going to help them out with the children."

"I would offer to help out, but my hands are pretty full with Constance and Chris. By the way, Chris was trying to walk today."

"Really? I want to be here when that happens. Maybe after supper I'll work with him on that. That boy needs to learn to walk soon. I need another helper on the construction site." Pete laughed, put his arms around Quinelle as she was washing and sterilizing baby bottles.

"Momma told me that she received a letter from Coot today. He is out of basic training and on to Ohio," Pete said.

"I sure do miss him. I hope he's happy."

"Me, too. It would have been so great if he could have gotten stationed here at Robins Air Force Base."

"Yea....but you know we have to trust God. He sees the bigger picture. There's a reason."

"I know. I know. Uh-oh, I hear some babies crying. I'll go get them and keep them occupied while you fix supper."

"Don't forget to change their diapers first."

"You don't have to remind me."

"Yes, I do, too!"

She could hear the laughter and the giggles from Pete and the kids. They were always so happy to see him at the end of the day, and likewise with Pete. He was just a big kid himself.

She thinks to herself: I hope our house is always full of laughter.

Chapter 31

1953 – the year for boys! All three of them – Willene, Etheel and Quinelle – had baby boys. Willene and Charles named their son, Charley; Etheel and Nathaniel named their son, Freddy; and Pete and Quinelle have Christopher. Their children will have plenty of cousins to grow up with.

Betty's family, David, Lucille, and Quinelle's family are together quite a bit. They all miss Lamar and Nathaniel's families. Coot is sorely missed too, especially by his Momma.

Family gatherings are never dull or boring. There are now eight children among us. When Nathaniel and Etheel and Lamar and Martha can join us, then there are eleven children! It can get quite loud and boisterous, but they do have fun. Being in this family brings back a lot of good memories growing up with her cousins. In spite of the financial difficulties and lacking for many things, we were happy in the Clark household.

David, Lucille and Pete's family attend church together. Betty and Robert attend a small church in the community where they live in Cochran Field. The Church of God the Stokes' attend is a small church located on the "main drag" in Warner Robins. Pete and Quinelle immediately joined the choir and have gotten involved in different ministries of the church. Another family in the church, the Barker family, are an integral part of this church. They have many family members attending. As the Stokes family grew and became members of this church, some called the church the "Stokes and Barker church"! Pete and Quinelle truly love their church and the people there.

A woman by the name of Esther Holland attends their church. She has been widowed for some years now. She has taken Quinelle under her wing, and is wanting her to assist her in the children's church ministry of the church. She told her she was not ready for that yet; maybe when the children got a little older.

Sister Holland, (they call each other sister or brother in our church), is so very devout. Pete and Quinelle have leaned on her for advice and understanding of the Scriptures. She's almost like a prophetess, but has never claimed to be one. She has counseled Pete in making decisions regarding his business dealings. She relays to them what God has spoken to her.

The teachings of the church are very strict, especially for women in regards to dress and appearance as godly women. Lots of "hell, fire and brimstone" preaching! In the community, they are known as the "holy rollers." Quinelle believes in the teachings of the church, but was still very confused at times. Sister Holland doesn't condemn her for her questions, but implores her to take time to study the scriptures for herself, and ask God for understanding and wisdom. She is like a Mother to Quinelle.

Pete is once again teaching a Sunday School class. Quinelle is very proud to be a part of this church family and the Stokes' family. Her life journey with Willie Furman has been quite adventuresome so far! Only God knows what the future holds. She knows no matter what that may be, she was learning to trust God.

Chapter 32

Five years later......
October 1958

"Mother, it's Constance, the house is on fire!"

"What did you say??" Quinelle screamed into the phone.

"I just came in from school. The house is on fire. Evelyn told me to call you."

"Where is Evelyn?"

"She ran outside with Chris and Mike. She told me to call you. The smoke is coming into the den."

"Go outside with Evelyn. I'll call the fire department." Quinelle went into panic mode. She was at Pete's office where she now worked. "Ann, call Pete on the radio and tell him the house is on fire. I'll call the fire department." She could hardly breathe. She prayed quietly that God would keep her family safe.

"Ann, I'm going home. When you hear from Pete, tell him to meet me there."

"Do you want me to drive you?" Ann had been working for Stokes Bros. Construction as the bookkeeper and they had made her feel like one of the family.

"No, just stay here and take care of things."

Quinelle couldn't believe what was happening. Why? How? What started a fire? Evelyn, the housekeeper, was a smoker. She had been told to always go outside to smoke, and had always abided by that rule. Or, had she? Oh, my children! My house! Lord, help me!!

With all these thoughts going through her head, she began to shake and cry. The car just wouldn't go fast enough.

Getting closer to their house that they had purchased just a couple of years ago, she could see smoke, but hadn't heard any fire trucks yet. Where are they?

This house was a big step for them. The home they had purchased in 1952 was only two bedrooms. Since they now had the two children, they were wanting more space. They wanted a three bedroom house in the Miller Elementary School district since Constance would be starting school in the fall of '58. Pete and his Dad built this house. She couldn't believe their good fortune in being able to make this purchase.

Coot had completed his enlistment in the Air Force. In 1956 while stationed in Ohio, he met Betty Sauls, a local girl. In 1957 they married and were transferred to Alaska; then in July 1958 their daughter, Sandy was born. They had just recently moved to Warner Robins. Coot and Pete decided to start their own construction company and to, also, open up a cabinet shop. Their Dad was very talented in building cabinets. Lamar and his family had moved to Warner Robins in 1955, and he and Pete had opened up an independent insurance agency. Business was good; both the building and insurance business.

As Quinelle approached the house, the street was blocked by on-lookers. She couldn't get to the house by car, so she jumped out of her car and started running up the hill toward the house. She saw Pete running toward her. She could hardly see for the tears streaming down her face.

"Pete!" Quinelle fell into his arms and collapsed.

"Quinelle, the children are okay. They are in the Cromer's yard across the street. The fire trucks have not arrived yet. Ann contacted me by radio and was told that a train has delayed them. They can't cross the tracks! The only fire station is on the Air Force Base."

Pete tried to console her as he was trying to control his emotions. He had to be strong for her; she knew that.

"Come on, Quinelle. The kids are asking for you."

Pete, Quinelle and the kids stood across the street and watched their dream home burn to the ground. By the time the fire trucks arrived, the house was a total loss.

They all huddled together and cried. The neighbors were trying to console the family, and offered to help in any way they could.

"Evelyn, what happened?" Pete could see that she was visibly shaken. She was lighting up one cigarette after the other. She kept them in her apron at all times.

"Constance had just gotten in from school. She ran upstairs and told me the boys were playing with matches and had caught the clothes on fire hanging in their closet downstairs. By the time we came downstairs, the whole closet was in flames. I grabbed Chris and Mike and headed to the door. (Mike was Betty's (Coot's wife) nephew, Chris' playmate for the day). I told Constance to use the phone downstairs and call Mrs. Stokes."

"Thanks for getting the kids out safely. You may go on home. We will be in touch with you. I don't know what we are going to do......" Pete's voice trailed off.

Evelyn hugged Quinelle and the children and said her good-byes.

Everything was gone – the new furniture, the piano, her sewing machine – thank goodness for insurance on the house.

These things could be replaced, but not the pictures.....It was almost too much to bear.

Lamar arrived as soon as he heard the news. Ann, at the office, had called him and told him what had happened.

Coot arrived shortly thereafter along with his Dad. Ann had reached them by radio as well while they were on the construction site.

Coot and Betty lived only a quarter of a mile away from

Pete and Quinelle. Coot invited them to stay in their home until they could figure out what to do.

"What are we going to do about clothes?" Quinelle wailed and put her face in her hands.

"We will figure it out, Quinelle. Let's go to Coot and Betty's and try to think clearly."

"Daddy," Pete said, "would you drive my truck over to Coot's? I'll drive over with Quinelle in our car."

"Sure, no problem. I'll take the kids with me."

The fire trucks were leaving the premises now. They had cordoned off the property with police tape. The fire chief told Pete he would be in contact with him when it was safe to go on the property and search for anything salvageable.

Pete and Quinelle descended the hill to their car. Quinelle couldn't help but look back at her devastated home; the smoke billowing overhead. Why did this happen to us? What's the reason, Lord? Help me get through this.

Pete held her tight as she sobbed uncontrollably. He tried to think of something to say to help ease the pain.

"Well," he said, "at least you were wearing your best suit today. You always look so pretty in it."

"Pete, you are amazing! You always seem to find the silver lining, and I love you for that." Quinelle climbed into the car and resolved to make the best of her situation.

When Quinelle made up her mind to do something, she trusted Jesus to help her find a way to make it happen.

Chapter 33

I smell smoke. Anytime I smell smoke my heart starts racing. Frantically, I look around the room, then raise up my head to look outside of *the picture window.* I don't see smoke, but I smell smoke. Am I dreaming again?

"Pete! Pete!"

"Coming – hang on," Pete answered from the kitchen.

"Is anything on fire? I smell smoke!" I don't know if he heard me. My voice is so weak.

Pete came into the living room with a dishtowel over his shoulder and said, "Yes, you smell smoke. I burned the toast, but everything is under control."

"You know how paranoid I get when I smell smoke."

"I'm sorry. How about some toast? I'll try not to burn it this time!" Pete laughed.

"I was thinking about the time our house burned down. That was one of the worst days of my life. Every time, no matter where I was, if I saw smoke in the direction of our home, I had to drop what I was doing and get home. Remember?"

"Oh, yeah, I remember......."

"We were planning a visit to Savannah to see Pearlene and Eddie, their son, Mike, and Pam was a newborn. Our house burning put everything on hold. I was so looking forward to that visit."

"Yoo-hoo", Mama softly uttered as she entered the living room.

"Come on in," Pete said.

"How are you this morning, Quinelle?"

"Okay, I woke up to the smell of burnt toast." I winked at Pete.

"I smelled it, too. How about I fix you some toast and I promise I won't burn it?" Mama chuckled.

"Sounds good."

Mama left for the kitchen.

"Etheel will be here in about an hour to help you get ready for your visit with Etta Mae."

"I can't wait to see her. It has been so long. Etta Mae – my very best friend in high school!"

"I'll go help MaMa in the kitchen. I'll juice you some watermelon."

As Pete leaves the room, I turn toward *the picture window* – again. A beautiful day with the wind gently blowing the trees. Lord, I pray, give me strength today to enjoy my visit with Etta Mae. I really don't feel well today. I seem to get weaker with each day. I don't know how much longer I can linger. I pray to God to heal me, as does my family, but, I'm tired, Lord.

Etheel arrived, and quickly washed my hair and rolled it. I dozed while sitting under the hair dryer. Hair done, makeup applied and dressed all with the help of my dear sister-in-law. What would I do without her?

"She's here!" Pete announced. "You sit right there, sweetheart. I'll go to the door."

Finally! She is here. I need to see her!

I couldn't just sit when Etta Mae walked into the room. I gathered all my strength, stood up, and embraced her. It was quite a while before we let go of one another. Pete stepped behind me to catch me if he needed to. The tears freely came as we cried together and laughed at the same time.

"Pete, it's such a beautiful day; I think we should sit out on the deck," I said as I hooked one arm around Pete's arm, and the other arm around Etta Mae's.

It was so good to sit and reminisce about our high school days. Etta Mae was the best friend a girl could have ever had. I was quiet around others, but I could tell her my dreams and secrets. She was the liaison between myself and Pete. She and Pete rode the school bus together for a time until he quit school. They, also, worked in the cotton fields together as their family's homes were very near to one another. Pete would give notes to Coot, who in turn would give them to Etta Mae while on the bus ride to school; then Etta Mae would pass the note on to me. Etta Mae swore to me she never read them. I believed her.

"There were lots of dreaming going on in those cotton fields, weren't there, Quinelle?" Etta Mae reminded her. "And a lot of those dreams have come true!"

"That's true," Quinelle reflected, "we knew the only way out of those cotton fields was to study hard and do well in school. We were both determined to do so."

"You both were so smart and being honor graduates; I was so proud of the both of you when you gave your speeches at your graduation ceremony." Pete interjected, as he rose from his chair. He leaned over and kissed me on my forehead, "I'm going to leave you two alone for a while, okay?"

"Okay."

As Pete walked away, Etta Mae took hold of my hand, and said, "Nell, you were always the kindest and sweetest person to everyone. If you had a dime, I knew that I had a nickel."

"Thanks for being my friend. We did have some good times even though we were 'underprivileged'!" Remember when we were on the way to our baccalaureate service that was held at church? Pete was given us a ride in that old Model A. It started leaking – whatever it was that was leaking, I don't remember – and choked down. Pete said he needed something to plug up the leak. He took his chewing gum that he had been chewing, and plugged up the hole, and on our way we went."

We laughed a lot that afternoon. It felt good to have a good belly laugh! Maybe this is the medicine I really need.

"You and Pete have a beautiful place here and a beautiful life together. God has truly blessed you both so much," Etta Mae exclaimed as she stood up and looked out over the pond behind the house.

"Yes, we have. I was hoping to grow old here with Pete. I wish I had more time with him. My only regret is that his work in building those convenient stores around the state, took him away from me much of the time. I would have rather have had him home."

"Pete has been a wonderful husband. Remember when Aunt Daisy asked you if there was anything else you would rather be doing than to marry Pete before she would agree to sign the marriage license?"

"Oh, yes, I remember. I told her that my mind was clear, and marrying Pete was what I wanted to do. I loved him so much. He was my first love, you know."

Etta Mae laughed. "I was remembering when you and Pete went to get your blood tests for the marriage license. You were in Dr. Moses' office located in the back of Big Martin's drugstore....."

"And, I fainted." They both giggled like old times.

I hated to see our time together come to an end. I knew that this would probably be the last time I would see Etta Mae, this side of heaven. Unless.....the miracle we were all praying for.....became a reality.

Pete helped me back inside the house and into bed. I was so exhausted and exhilarated at the same time.

Pete walked Etta Mae to her car, and hugged her neck. "You were, and still are 'my cotton-pickin' buddy. Thanks so much for making the effort to see Quinelle. She needed this today."

Etta Mae's tears were now flowing in full force. "I'll always remember how much she loved people and loved the Lord.

She was always such a positive person; never complaining about her situation, losing her Mother at such a young age, and her Dad never being around much. She is still that same loving and positive person today. You have been blessed, Pete Stokes."

Letting the tears go, he said "I know." The lump in his throat prevented him from saying more.

Chapter 34

"You have a baby girl!" announced the nurse as the doctor delivered Pete and Quinelle's third child in April of 1961.

"Well, Connie will be thrilled to have a baby sister. Chris was wanting a brother," Pete said with laughter in his voice. "I'll call Daddy. He's at the office and the kids should be there soon from school. He said he would stay there with them until I got home."

"Are we still going to name her Gwendolyn Monica?" asked Pete.

"Yes, but let's call her Gwen. You know how we called Connie, Constance, but when she started school, her name somehow got shortened to Connie. We might as well shorten Gwendolyn's now!" Quinelle stated.

Pete nodded with approval.

"When I get home, I'll call your sisters and let them know you had the baby."

"Thanks, Pete. I'm so tired. I think I would like to take a nap before they bring Gwen in for her feeding."

"I'll call you later. I'll be back in the morning as soon as the kids are in school. I love you, Quinelle."

"I love you, too, Pete, and I always will!"

As Pete exited the room, Quinelle's thoughts turned to how their lives were going to be different with this new baby.

It had been eight years since their last child was born. This baby was a surprise, to say the least; but a nice surprise. They both had looked forward to this day.

Pete had moved his office into their home. That made her life much simpler. She was able to help out with the office work while attending to her house, and was able to be home when Connie and Chris got home from school.

They had recently moved – again – to a house that Pete built, of course. The new house had a sunken living room, which was the new fad. She loved the purple carpet she had chosen. She especially liked their new neighbors, Roy and Jean Lifsey. They had a daughter just a couple of years younger than Chris. Her name was Connie, also. Jean and she had become really close. It was so nice to have a dear friend right next door.

She thanked God for a safe delivery and a healthy baby girl. She asked God to help Chris with the disappointment of a baby sister instead of a baby brother. She grinned at that thought; then succumbed to a much-needed nap.

Chapter 35

Morris, Quinelle's only brother, died in September 1963. This news came about a month before their move to Brunswick, Georgia. Two events in her life that were very troublesome. She wasn't sure Morris was prepared to meet his Maker, and this move to Brunswick was testing her faith.

Pete felt a call from God to move to Brunswick and to assist in a church located there. He wasn't even sure which church, but knew he was to go. When he told Quinelle about this "call", she couldn't begin to imagine what they were going to have to undertake to make this move happen. What about the business? What about the children and school? What about family and friends? What would they think? After much soul-searching and prayer, she acquiesced to her husband's bidding, and trusted God to lead them in the right direction.

Pete's Mom and Dad, David and Lucille, decided to move, also. David would help Pete start a cabinet shop business in Brunswick. They traveled to Brunswick and found homes to rent, and a building to rent for the cabinet shop. David's sister and brother-in-law, Lucy and Casey Monsees, resided in Brunswick at that time. That was a plus!

The move was made in October 1963. This was a tremendous undertaking for Quinelle with a two year old. Lucille was an enormous help with the children. Connie and Chris had to get enrolled in a new school right away. They were not very happy leaving their current school and friends. Quinelle prayed for her children to make new friends quickly and easily. She prayed, also, to locate a piano teacher for Connie, so she could continue her lessons.

She also prayed that God would lead them speedily to the church they were supposed to minister and serve in whatever capacity they were needed. She prayed for Pete's business to be successful. She trusted God fully to take care of their needs and wants. This step of faith they had already taken had made them both stronger in their walk with Jesus. There wasn't a lot of money when this move took place, just a lot of faith!

"Hey, Pete," Quinelle said as she ran to his side, "Look what I've found!" They were both walking around the perimeter of their new home. Connie and Chris were playing hide and seek with Gwen.

"A diamond ring!" she exclaimed. "I found it in this clump of grass over there near the fence."

"I wonder if it's worth anything," Pete said as he examined the ring.

"We could take it to a jeweler in town and see, couldn't we?"

"I suppose. But first, let's call the landlord and find out who lived here prior, and see if they lost the ring."

"You're right. I'll go in the house right now and make that phone call."

As Quinelle made her way to the telephone, she thought how wonderful it would be if that ring wasn't claimed, the money they could possibly get for it. The ring was beautiful, but they could certainly use found money right now.

She could hear the laughter and giggles from the children outside. They will be okay, she surmised. Connie and Chris seem to be adjusting to their new school. They rode the bus to school. It seemed to help matters that there was the two of them, not just one going it alone.

Gwen would accompany Quinelle to the cabinet shop daily where Quinelle helped out with the paperwork and bookkeeping. Connie and Chris rode the bus to the shop from school.

Our search for "the" church landed us at the Southside Church of God in Brunswick. This was the one that God led us to. The church was struggling not only financially, but seemingly had no life. The pastor, Eddie Green, needed some new members that could take on leadership roles. A leader and prayer warrior was needed. Pete Stokes was that man!

After several minutes Quinelle rushed back outside. "Pete, I talked with our landlord. He gave me the name of the couple that rented before us; but all he knows is that they were being transferred to another base somewhere in Alabama, and doesn't know how or where to reach them. He suggests we take the approach of 'finders keepers, loosers weepers'. He says they never mentioned to him about losing a ring."

"Do you want to keep the ring, Quinelle? It sure is beautiful and you don't even own a wedding band."

"No, let's see what we can get for it. We could certainly use the money."

"I'll take it to a pawn shop on Monday and see what I can get for it."

Quinelle ran back into the house and placed the ring in a safe place. Thank you, Jesus, for finding this ring. I just know it's worth something.

Chapter 36

It is now November 1963. The President of the United States, John F. Kennedy, has been assassinated. Connie and Chris ran in the house after getting off the school bus and told of how they spent most of the day in their classrooms watching the news.

Quinelle, too, had been watching the television most of the day while preparing for a visit from her sisters and her Dad. They had seen each other just a couple of months back at Morris' funeral. Lois drove up from Florida and met up with Willene and Pearlene in Savannah. Daddy had been visiting with Willene for a few days. Willene, through the years, had the most contact with our Daddy. An appointment had been scheduled for their Dad at the VA Hospital in Dublin; so they decided to all ride up together to get him to the hospital. This was a first, having all her sisters and her Dad to visit in her home all at one time. This trip together was, also, a first for the girls and their Dad.

Quinelle had never spent much time with her sister, Lois. Lois had married and moved to Florida shortly after Quinelle was born. As a matter of fact, she didn't really even know Lois. As the years progressed, Lois would attend Aunt Daisy's birthday dinners, and for the most part, that would be the only time Quinelle would see her elder sister.

This time spent with their Dad was much needed and was

a time of forgiveness for past offences. After all these years, their Dad was still their Dad – no matter the past.

While Quinelle was gone for the day, Pete was packing again – for the second time since moving to Brunwick.

He had decided he wanted to move to the island – St. Simons Island – after their six months' lease ended on the house in Brunswick. So, they packed up again and made the move. A new house and near the beach was exciting for the children. No schools on the island, so Quinelle would have to take Connie and Chris to school every day, then on to the cabinet shop with Gwen.

A couple of weeks later, while the kids were in school, the moving van moved the household goods over to the new house.

The children were ecstatic to be so close to the ocean!

"Why can't we go to the beach?" Chris lamented to his Mother.

"Let me finish unpacking these boxes first. Why don't you go outside and play?" Quinelle said as she patted him on the head. "I promise, we will go later today."

"Okay." The oak trees were huge in their yard. Chris decided a fun thing to do would be to climb a tree.

Connie remained in the house to help. Quinelle put Gwen down for a nap, so now she can get something done.

"Mother, help!" Chris was screaming at the top of his lungs.

"What in the world?" Quinelle thought as she and Connie ran outside to see what the matter was.

The lady next door heard the screams, also, and was standing under the large oak tree, when Quinelle realized where Chris was.

Chris had indeed climbed up in the tree, but now realized that he couldn't get down. The neighbor lady was a tall, hefty woman and offered to reach up to Chris. He placed his feet on her shoulders as she lowered him to the ground. That's how they were introduced to the neighbor!

Chris was visibly shaken. "How about you and me search the yard? We might just find another $700 diamond ring!" Quinelle laughed as she hugged Chris tightly.

The summer on the island was filled with many trips over to the beach. Quinelle still had to go to the cabinet shop most days to work, with the children in tow.

So, late afternoons and Saturdays, the Stokes family could usually be found at the beach.

This move to St. Simons was short-lived. By the end of the summer, Pete was sure God was telling him that his work was done at the Southside Church of God. The church had grown, not only in numbers, but spiritually. There were now members that could help carry on the business of the church, too.

By the middle of August 1964, they were packing up and moving back to Warner Robins. They needed to get back in time to register the kids for school. No more beach!! The kids were not happy about that, but did look forward to being back with their cousins and their friends.

Quinelle had a lot of mixed emotions. A lot had happened in twelve months! Two houses, getting involved in a new church, starting up a new cabinet shop business, getting the kids back and forth to school, taking care of a baby, getting Connie to piano lessons, practicing the piano to play at church – so much had been done. Just the thought of packing up again was overwhelming. On the other hand, she was excited about the move back to Warner Robins. She had missed their church there; her friends and Pete's family. She was hoping this would be the last move for a long while. Well, so much for that thought......

Chapter 37

Three houses in two years! Quinelle just thought her moving days were over.

While residing in the second home since moving back to Warner Robins, Pete built them a new home on the south side of town. This house was different from all others; this one had an inground swimming pool. This is something Quinelle had never dreamed of having, but Pete had. But, the best part about this move is that they would be back in the same neighborhood they were in prior to their move to Brunswick. Pete and Quinelle's best friends, Roy and Jean Lifsey and their daughter, Connie Sue, still lived here. They were next door neighbors for many years, and became the best of friends.

The building business in Warner Robins was booming. J.N. and Etheel had moved to Warner Robins back in 1958, and had joined in the family construction business. They now have five children; Larry, Tarrell, Freddy, Nancile, and Tommy. Pete and Coot (who now wants to be called Freeman- his first name), are also in the real estate business, calling their company Paramount Realty. Freeman and Betty now have three children – Sandy, Steve and Kim.

J.N. or Nathaniel (his nieces and nephews call him Uncle Nathaniel), being familiar with heavy equipment, would usually do the grading of the lot prior to construction of a new home with a John Deere crawler. Nathaniel eventually purchased the crawler and other heavy equipment and began his own grading business.

Lamar was now an insurance agent with Nationwide Insurance. His office was located next to the construction company and real estate office of his brothers. Lamar and Martha have a large brood of six children – Jessi, Linda, Elaine, Lamar, Jr., Paulette, and Dennis.

Pete's sister, Betty and her husband, Robert, had moved to Warner Robins from Cochran Field. They have three children – Diane, Calvin, and David. Pete's parents, David and Lucille, had recently moved into a house in the same neighborhood as Pete and Quinelle. The entire Stokes family all now resided in Warner Robins, What a blessed and large(!) family they were, too.

Quinelle's sister, Willene, and her family were now stationed at Robins AFB. What a blessing that was! Willene's two children, Carolyn and Charley, came over often to visit with Connie and Chris. The cousins enjoyed each other's company so very much. There were numerous sleepovers! Charles had moved his family to England with him for the previous three years while he was stationed there with the Air Force. Quinelle was overjoyed to have her sister nearby again.

Pearlene had married in 1956 to Eddie Smith, a man she met in Savannah while living with Willene and Charles. They now have three children – Mike, Pam, and Angie. They still reside in Savannah; so they are close enough to visit on some weekends.

Lois, the eldest sister, still lives in Florida with her husband, Wes. They come to Aunt Daisy's birthday dinners that are still held every June. Sometimes, they make it to Warner Robins for Thanksgiving.

Morris, the only brother, who died in 1963, had a grandson born while he was on his deathbed. Ann, his daughter, and her son, Bill reside in Vidalia.

Things were going pretty well in Uvalda, too. Quinelle's

cousin, Georgia and her brothers, Bill, Harry, and Nick, were now all married and having children. Aunt Daisy and Uncle Otis were enjoying life and all the grandchildren.

Quinelle had so much to be thankful for. Both Pete's family and her family were Christians and loved the Lord. God had been so good!

Chapter 38

Looking out *the picture window* I see a dreary, cloudy spring day. I couldn't help myself today with thoughts of despair. All I seem to think about these days are the past. I don't think I have a future here any longer.

"Pete, I was just thinking about the Christmases spent with your siblings and their families all these years. The first couple of Christmases we all gathered at our little house on Peachtree Circle. The family grew so large and so fast we had to start meeting in the church social hall on at the Houston Road Church of God. I'm going to miss those family times. I'm so glad to have been a part of your family."

"Quinelle, where's your faith? You talk as if you are not going to be here this Christmas." Pete was struggling to keep his voice from wavering. He had to be strong for her.

"I'm not giving up, Pete, but sometimes I need to express my feelings and thoughts, or I feel as if I will burst." With that statement, she began to cry.

Pete held her in his arms as she sobbed. "You have been so strong, sweetheart, just keep trusting God to heal you, and rest in your faith."

"If faith is rest, why are we struggling so?"

I turn my back to the picture window. I can't stand this pain much longer. I want to be strong in my faith. But, this is reality. I just want to die. I'm just existing here in front of this window. I want to escape.

Pete pulled the covers up over me. I was so cold and shivering. I'm too tired to say thank you, but he knows. He will sit on the bed rubbing my back until I go to sleep, as the usual.

MaMa entered the room as Quinelle drifted off to sleep. "Anything I can do, Pete?"

"No, she's gone back to sleep. She doesn't stay awake much at the time anymore."

He followed his Mother back into the kitchen. She had prepared them something to eat.

"Do you think she made the right decision to discontinue the chemo treatments?"

"I don't know, but after a few treatments making her so sick, she told me 'if this is living, I don't want to live'. I couldn't blame her and certainly couldn't make that decision for her."

"I pray constantly for her, Pete."

"I know you do, Momma. Thanks for all you do." With that, he gave her a big bear hug. They cried together.

Chapter 39

Summer 1968

"Here we are," announced Pete as he pulled the car with the travel trailer in tow into the entrance of Vogel State Park.

"Okay, kids, you know not to run off as soon as we get parked. We need your help in getting things set up," Quinelle reminded them. She was as excited as the kids were. Finally, she thought to herself, time away!!

It was like pulling teeth to get Pete away from his work. She talked him into purchasing this travel trailer so they could go camping, mostly in the North Georgia mountains. This was her favorite place to camp. There were lots of activities to keep the children busy – putt-putt, paddle boats, fishing, swimming and campfire sing-alongs. This time away from home gave her the opportunity to catch up on her reading, and to do some fishing. Quinelle dearly loved to fish. Many Saturday mornings she would wake the kids up very early, and spend the rest of the day fishing in a nearby pond or lake. Pete was always working. Sometimes MaMa and Granddaddy would go with us. She taught the kids how to fish and how to clean them, also. Her dream was to have a fishing pond in her backyard!

This particular trip Chris brought a friend as did Gwen. Gwen, being so much younger than Connie and Chris, who were now 15 and 16 years of age, was not included in some of their activities such as scoping out members of the opposite sex! They didn't want a little sister tagging along. Quinelle thought Gwen having a friend to play with would help her out, too.

"Oh, this mountain air, Pete, I needed this," Quinelle said as she wrapped her arms around him. "I know this will help my sinuses."

"This trip will also get you off that sewing machine for a while, too. I hope Connie and Gwen appreciate the clothes you make for them. You were always good with that sewing machine, even making your own dresses when you were in high school. I still remember that peach colored dress you made to get married in." Pete returned her hug with a kiss – right on the lips.

"Remember where we are, Pete Stokes. Let me get your mind in the right direction. We need to set up camp for cooking our supper."

"Okay, boys, let's go gather some firewood. You girls help your Mother."

Quinelle enjoyed spending this time with her family. These trips gave her the time to reflect on her life and brought back memories of simpler times gone by. The cool mountain breezes were most welcome, especially when the temperatures were in the nineties when they left Middle Georgia that afternoon. What a relief!

"How great is our God!" Quinelle said aloud to no one in particular. These mountains always seemed to bring her closer to God.

Chapter 40

"Can you believe we are grandparents? How quickly things change?!" Quinelle exclaimed to Pete as they left the hospital.

"I don't feel like a grandpa!" Pete countered. "Boy, it's been a long day waiting for that little girl to get here."

"I know Connie was exhausted!"

They drove the rest of the way home in silence, mostly from weariness of the waiting for their granddaughter to be born, and, also, from the mental exhaustion of concern for their daughter's well-being.

Quinelle was thinking back over the last two years – the ups and downs in their family that had transpired. Connie had graduated from high school in May 1970 and left for college in September 1970. Chris graduated from high school a year later, and never came back home. He and Pete did not see eye-to-eye, to say the least. After attending one year of college, Connie married and a few months later had their first grandchild.

They were not thrilled about the marriage and the man she chose to marry. Wayne would not have been the man they would have chosen. He was not a Christian, didn't even attend church. He looked like the common "hippie" – long hair and all! What was Connie thinking? Quinelle was more disappointed in that fact that she had thrown away the opportunity to attend college; something Quinelle had wanted for herself and was unable to do so. She wanted this so much for Connie.

Connie had taken piano lessons all through her school years. Quinelle made sure of that. She even took piano lessons herself with her while she was in high school. They helped each other out with their lessons. Connie was planning on being a music major. Quinelle was so excited that she was going to pursue this path of study. Now, everything had changed!

Quinelle was really missing her son, too. He was very rarely seen. Her heart had been broken twice now.

Chapter 41

1973

Moving day again! The excitement of moving to the "country" with several fishing ponds overshadowed the task of the actual packing up and all the work involved. Quinelle and Pete had bought some acreage in South Houston County, a small community named Haynesville, and were in the process of building a new home. The house has not been completed just yet, but they decide to go ahead and move closer, and live on the property in a mobile home. Oh, Quinelle thought to herself, I will be able to fish every day! They stored the majority of their household goods; the living room furniture ended up temporarily in Connie's house since she had no furniture in her living room.

Chris had married; he and Pete had made amends, and were working together on building this new home.

This was Quinelle's dream come true. God had truly blessed them through the years. There were good times and some hard times along the way, but they always trusted God to supply their needs. God, also, took care of some of their wants along the way, and this was one of them; a new home outside city life with fishing ponds!

"I've got lunch ready for all you boys," Quinelle announced as she brought sandwiches out on the newly built deck of the new house. She didn't have to say that but once!

Once lunch was devoured, Chris decided to do a little

fishing before going back to work. He loved to fish just as much as his Mother. This was late Fall with a slight constant wind blowing throughout the day. Casting his fishing line into the water, the wind caught it and propelled it into a tree limb overhanging the pond. Chris tried to yank it out of the tree but was unsuccessful. He decided to climb out onto the limb and retrieve his line and his valued fishing lure. Just as he was about to grab the line, the tree limb broke, and into the chilly water he went! Quinelle and Pete were watching this episode, and had a good belly laugh, which lasted for a long time. Quinelle brought Chris a shirt and pair of pants belonging to Pete to wear while she dried his clothes. Quinelle had another good laugh watching Chris work while in clothes too big for him.

As Pete and Quinelle were getting ready to retire after a full day, Pete said, "It sure is good to have my son working with me again. I have surely missed him so."

"Our prayers have been answered, Pete, in so many ways. Chris has changed quite a bit since he married and expecting their first child – another grandbaby for us. It's good to see Connie and our granddaughter, Neilie, when they come for their weekly visit, and Gwen seems to be adapting pretty well to our moving. I pray when she changes schools next school year that she will make friends quickly and easily."

Quinelle had had a very busy day. Unpacking boxes for their temporary move into the mobile home, which was located just across the pond from the new house, and driving quite a distance getting Gwen to school and back. And tomorrow would be more of the same, as she drifted off to sleep with a smile on her face.

Chapter 42

"Another granddaughter," Quinelle reported to Pete as she hung up the phone from the hospital. "That was Wayne. Connie went into labor this morning while at the hospital for a test, and had the baby before noon."

"Well, happy birthday to me! She said she wanted to have the baby on my birthday," Pete responded.

"It won't take me but a few minutes to get ready to go to the hospital. Are you coming with me?"

"Of course, I'm coming with you!" Pete hugged her and with a teasing smirk on his face, "Your still looking pretty good for an old Grandma!"

She lingered in his arms. Looking up into his face, she said, "You don't look so bad yourself. Happy Birthday, Grandpa!"

Riding to the hospital, Quinelle was thinking how quickly their lives were changing. This was Connie's second child, and Chris had a son. Gwen was a teenager – where did the time go?

She and Pete were enjoying their new home, and were attending the Assembly of God Church in Clinchfield – an even smaller community near Haynesville. The church was very small and needed someone to help them. They believed that this was another mission for them authored by God. It wasn't long that Pete had the church in a building program. Property was purchased in Haynesville and Pete built them a new church building! Quinelle was playing the piano for the congregation, and began a children's church program and an adult choir. She, also, initiated a library of books, videos and tapes she shared with the members. The church was prospering and many souls were saved. The pastor, Gene McKinney and his wife, Laverne, had been blessed beyond their expectations.

God had blessed the Stokes family once again with a church family that they loved, and that loved them.

Chapter 43

The birds awake me with their insistent chirping. What a beautiful blue sky has welcomed me this morning as I peer through *the picture window*. I actually feel like singing. I'm thinking of the song with the words – what a day of rejoicing that will be. When we all see Jesus, we'll sing and shout the victory!

I hope this will be one of my good days.....

"Good morning, Sunshine," Pete exclaims as he enters the room. "I opened the curtains so that when you woke up you could see how beautiful it is outside."

"Thanks, it is such as glorious day."

Pete leaned over and gave me a kiss on my forehead. Taking my hand in his, he told me how much he loved me. He then prayed for me to have a good day today, and that my body would be healed by the stripes of Jesus.

"Remember today is Saturday. I'm sure the kids and grandkids will be stopping by sometime today to see you."

"Pete, I'm not sure how much longer I want the grandchildren to see me in my condition. I want them to remember me as I was."

"Well, let's not think about that right now, okay? You seem to be feeling better today, so maybe a visit will be good for you."

"I hope they don't wait too late to come see me."

"I'll call them and tell them that is what you prefer. In the meantime I'll get you some breakfast."

Yesterday I had Etheel hand me the mirror after she fixed my hair. I could hardly believe the image I saw in that mirror. Was that me? I didn't like what I had seen.

No self-pity today, Quinelle, I tell myself. I'm going to cherish this feeling I have right now. I'm still here and I am loved by my husband and my family. God loves me. I feel that love, too.

I speak out loud to Him, my Lord and Saviour. Are you going to heal me? Today would be fine with me... if that is your plan for me. I accept whatever Your plan is.

Unbeknownst to Quinelle, her cousin, Georgia and her husband, Johnny were on their way to visit and were scheduled to arrive around noon. Pete was keeping this as a surprise.

Sitting on the couch, I heard a commotion in the kitchen; sounds of whispering voices.

"Nell."

No one calls me Nell anymore. I turned to see Georgia entering the living room.

"Oh my goodness. I can't believe my eyes," I said as she sat down beside me and wrapped her arms around me. We held each other for quite some time.

Pete and Johnny joined us. Johnny sat down on the other side of me, and hugged my neck.

"Pete didn't tell me you were coming."

"I thought I would surprise you", Pete said grinning from ear to ear. "A nice surprise, huh?"

"Oh, yes, I am so glad to see you. It's been close to a year now, at Aunt Daisy's birthday dinner last June."

"Why don't we all go out to the deck? It's so nice outside, and the sunshine will probably do you some good, Quinelle," Pete announced as he helped me off the couch.

Pete and Mama had prepared sandwiches for lunch. The sunshine did feel so good.

"How are all your family doing? How's Aunt Daisy?"

"Everyone is doing well. Momma and Daddy both said to tell you hello and that they love you," Georgia responded.

After lunch Pete and Johnny walked around the property while Georgia and I reminisced about the old days. We laughed and we cried together. What a wonderful "sister" she has been to me since the day Pearlene and I showed up at their home, and lived together as a family for the next eight years.

I told her Etta Mae had been here to see me recently.

"I would love to see her again. It's been so many years," Georgia said, "I think the last time I saw her was at your high school graduation."

Pete and Johnny returned to the deck. Johnny told Georgia that they needed to get back on the road and head home.

Our good-byes were bittersweet. Georgia telling me that she hopes to see me at the birthday dinner in June, and I know deep within my soul that I probably will never see her again in this lifetime.

Chapter 44

A doctor visit is scheduled for Quinelle. There is a lump in her breast, a very large lump. A lumpectomy is scheduled to determine if the lump is malignant or benign. The diagnosis: breast cancer. Surgery is performed immediately to remove the breast.

Arriving home from the hospital, Quinelle is subjected to visitors, none of which she really wants to see right now. She has been mutilated by the surgeon's knife, and is feeling less than a woman. She thanks the well-wishers and retreats to the privacy of her bedroom.

What have they done to me? She could barely move her arm. The pain was excruciating. Looking in the mirror at her chest, she now only has one breast. How funny does that look? I'm too embarrassed for Pete to see this, and I think he never shall.

Chemotherapy treatments are the doctor's orders beginning soon. He believes the mastectomy removed the cancer, but hopes to eradicate any more cancer in the future with the chemo treatments. The doctor told her if she remained cancer-free for the next five years, the possibility of cancer returning would be virtually nil.

As she gets into bed for some rest, she thinks of the grandchildren. She has been taking care of them for Connie and Chris during the week while they all worked. Chris divorced

Shane's mother and remarried. His present wife, Joann, has been a wonderful stepmother to Shane. They now have a son together, Luke, born last year.

She will be unable to take care of them for a time. She must take it easy for a few weeks.

"Gwen, come help me!" Quinelle mustered up enough strength to call out.

Gwen had just arrived home from school when she heard her Mother. Finding her Mother lying prostrate on the bathroom floor, she proceeded to help her to the couch.

"What can I do?" Gwen asked.

"Please bring me a cold rag."

At that moment Pete walked into the room. "What is going on?"

"I've been vomiting again from this chemo treatment I had this morning. I hate this!"

Pete places the cold rag on Quinelle's forehead. She is writhing back and forth holding the rag on her face.

"Just try to calm down, sweetheart. This will pass."

"Never again. I have made up my mind that there will be no more treatments. If this is living, then I don't want to live," she uttered adamantly. "I will trust God and God alone."

"Okay, as you wish."

Pete and Quinelle were praying for a miracle of healing before the doctor's diagnosis. They knew something was not right when the lump first appeared, but had prayed for God to intervene. He didn't. But, their faith was still strong and they were not going to give up. The prayer of faith now was that her recovery would be easy and speedy, and she would be totally healed of the disease of cancer.

Pete quoted many times the Bible verses, "...by His stripes we are healed." Isaiah 53:5. "Who forgives all your sins and heals all your diseases." Psalm 103:3.

Chapter 45

"Can you believe it? Our baby graduating from high school!" Quinelle said to Pete as she grasped his hand on the way out of the stadium after Gwen's graduation ceremony.

"Time has a way of moving right along very quickly, doesn't it? The past eighteen years have been quite eventful," Pete declared as he pulled her hand to his lips and kissed it.

"What are Gwen's plans for the rest of the afternoon and evening?" Pete asked.

"She is going over to Marilyn's house for a while, then they are meeting up with some friends, and are planning to go out to eat. She will be home by ten, she assured me."

"So, you mean, she has chosen to hang out with her friends rather than join the family for our weekly fish fry," Pete snickered. They both laughed.

"Remember, we need to stop by the fish market on the way home, and pick up some more fish for tonight. I took some out of the freezer earlier today to thaw, but what we caught this week will not be enough to feed us all," Quinelle reminded him.

"MaMa asked me this morning if we were still frying fish tonight. Boy, she does love fried fish and your hushpuppies. Daddy sure loved fishing and eating fish, didn't he? I sure do miss him."

Pete's Dad, David, and Mother (MaMa) had been living

with Pete and Quinelle for a couple of years when just last year, he passed away. He had been suffering with emphysema, and a couple of days before he died, he had told Pete he was not doing anybody any good in his condition. He was ready to go.

"The kids will be over around the usual time – six o'clock. I'll have some time to rest before the crew gets here," Quinelle breathed deeply.

"How are you feeling, sweetheart?"

"I'm okay, just need to take the time to rest a spell."

"Momma asked me what she could do to help with the meal tonight. She says we don't ever let her do anything. I think she just wants to feel needed," Pete said.

"Tell her she can make the coleslaw for me. The fixings are in the refrigerator."

As soon as they arrived home, Quinelle went upstairs to rest. Finally, she thought to herself, I can get out of this bra. It still was not comfortable even after two years after her surgery. She still couldn't bear to look at herself. She avoided that as much as she could. That was something that she wouldn't allow Pete to see either.

Follow-up visits to the doctor had been very positive. Of course, she was reprimanded by the doctor for declining the chemotherapy treatments. So far, so good.

The weekly fish fry had become a tradition at "Pete's Paradise. Fish were caught during the week and frozen. If not enough fish had been caught that week, then off to the fish market to purchase more. Mr. Spillers, the owner of the market, always laughed when he saw one of us coming in. He knew we had not had enough "luck" that week catching fish.

Life was good. All Quinelle's children and five grandchildren were living close by. Chris and Connie had houses built next door to one another in Haynesville. They all attended church together. Quinelle and her children performed special songs many times during the church worship services. Her prayers had been answered in that situation, and she was certainly hoping her prayers were being answered in regard to her health. Prayers that the cancer would never occur again.

Chapter 46

Thanksgiving 1980

"Guess what, Pete?" Quinelle posed to Pete as she hung up the phone after talking with her sister, Pearlene.

"What?"

"Lois is coming up for Thanksgiving this year. She is going to ride up from Savannah with Pearlene and Eddie. Isn't that wonderful?"

"Yes, I'm glad she can make it."

"Let's see – Charles and Willene, Charlie and his wife, Eddie and Pearlene, Ann and her son, Bill, Lois, Chris and Joanne with their three kids, Connie and her two, and Connie's fiancé, Lonnie, Gwen and Kevin, your Mother, and you and I - that makes twenty-three altogether for Thanksgiving dinner. Hope we have nice weather, so some can eat out on the deck."

Thanksgiving arrived with all the guests as planned. Quinelle enjoyed so much having her sisters here with her. It wasn't very often they were all together, especially with Lois. They usually only saw her at Aunt Daisy's birthday dinner each June. Lois still lived in Florida with her husband, Wes. She had a severely handicapped son that had required much of her time since his birth. He had recently been admitted to a nursing home for round-the-clock care.

Following the feast, a walk was in order. It was a beautiful day and walking around the ponds in the glorious sunshine was the remedy for the full stomachs. After the walk the young adults and the children decided to ride up to the softball field, which was located by the firehouse in Haynesville and play softball. This was the practice field for the mens' and womens' church softball teams for the two churches in Haynesville – the Assembly of God and the Baptist churches.

With the children and grandchildren off playing softball, Quinelle and her sisters spent the afternoon giggling and telling stories of days past while the men either watched football or napped.

The festivities are over. Everyone is headed back to their own "neck of the woods" as we say here in the South.

Quinelle decides to retire early. She is exhausted. Tomorrow is another busy day with the wedding tomorrow afternoon. The phone rings.

"Yes, Connie, what is it?" Quinelle asks while yawning.

"Mother, can you do me a favor? I totally forgot my wedding dress is a little too long. I really need it hemmed up," Connie said with anxiety in her voice.

"Okay. Just come on over and I'll take care of it." Quinelle thinks to herself – what would she do without me?

"Thanks, Mother, what would I do without you? Love you. Be right over."

The dress taken care of, Quinelle retraces her steps back up to the bedroom. Pete is already in the bed awaiting her arrival. He had kept the girls, Neilie and Heather, occupied while Quinelle hemmed Connie's dress.

"I know you are tired, Quinelle. Come on in and let me rub your back for you," Pete said as he throws back the covers for her.

"Thank. I'll take you up on that offer."

As she slid into bed, she laid on her stomach. Pete proceeded to massage her neck and shoulders. He sure loved his wife. He was so thankful she was doing so well physically.

"Another big day tomorrow, Pete. I hope Connie is making

a better decision than the last marriage. Also, taking on two stepchildren is an enormous challenge, especially since they will be in the household full-time. They don't ever see their Mother that lives in Texas."

"Well, we will just continue to pray for all of them," Pete said as he patted Quinelle on the backside.

"Let's pray right now, Pete."

They held hands and Pete led in a prayer of thanksgiving for all their blessings; asked God to bless all their children and grandchildren; thanked God for Quinelle's continued good health, and thanked Him for a good night's sleep.

Quinelle thought to herself as she was drifting off to sleep - thank you, Jesus, for this wonderful man I am married to. I am a happy and blessed woman.

Chapter 47

May 1981

"Our Gwendolyn getting married today – it is hard to fathom that our baby will not be coming back home today." Quinelle pondered as she straightened Pete's bowtie.

"I think she has made a good decision to marry Kevin. I really like him. He's a fine Christian young man. He seems to have his head on straight," Pete said as he reined Quinelle in for a hug.

"Careful now. Don't wrinkle my dress. I think we should be getting on over to the church."

"You look beautiful, Quinelle Stokes, and absolutely radiant today."

"Thanks, Pete, you're looking pretty handsome in that white suit," Quinelle cooed.

"We need to go," Gwen shouted from downstairs. She had her suitcase in hand, packed for the honeymoon. The plan was to put on her wedding dress at the church. "I want to make sure I get to the church before Kevin. I don't want him to see me before the wedding."

Pete took the suitcase from her and they headed to the car. The church was only five minutes away. They would be there before anyone else, he thought to himself.

Pete and Quinelle conversed quietly in their "waiting room" at the church awaiting the arrival of the bridesmaids and groomsmen.

"Two daughters getting married within the past six months... how fast things are changing in our world," Pete mused.

"Things sure have been different around the house since Neilie and Heather aren't staying with us anymore after school. Since Connie married and moved to Perry, their stepsister, Kim, is old enough to watch them until Connie gets in from work. I miss them living near us," Quinelle stated with a sadness in her voice.

"Well, you still help to take care of Chris' three kids a lot, and you see the girls at church and at our fish fry every week. It's not like they have moved a hundred miles away. And speaking of the little angels, here they are now."

Connie and Chris had arrived with their children, all of whom were part of the wedding party.

"Since I am the matron of honor, I am going to check on the bride," Connie said as she left the girls with their grandparents.

The wedding went off without a hitch, as we say here in "redneck country." Kevin and Gwen drove off amidst the rain of rice and confetti.

Arriving back home, Pete and Quinelle collapsed into their recliners.

Several minutes passed before either of them spoke. "Gwen looked so beautiful today, didn't she? Quinelle said sluggishly.

"Yes, and so happy, too!"

"It's not going to feel right around here without Gwen."

"You'll get used to it; just like you did when Connie left for college and when Chris left after graduation. Just think....we are empty-nesters now," Pete said with a triumphal voice.

"Just the two of us once again, but in a much, much bigger home than when we started out."

They both laughed at the memory of their first apartment.

"We have truly been blessed, Quinelle."

"Yes, we have." Quinelle paused. "We have been blessed with that motor home that is sitting in the garage waiting for those trips we are supposed to be taking. We need to plan a mountain trip real soon, don't we, Pete?"

Pete had promised Quinelle that they would do some traveling, especially to those mountains that she loved so much.

"Okay, okay. You're right. Let's do it!"

Chapter 48

Christmas 1981

The annual Stokes' family Christmas get-together was under-
way. Food and gifts were being brought in by the armfuls. This
was a joyous occasion for the Stokes family. Not only was it a
celebration of Jesus' birth, but it was another opportunity for
the family to come together for some fun and fellowship, not
to mention all the good food!

The Stokes family had grown by leaps and bounds. The
first cousins were now having children of their own. No longer
were these celebrations able to be held in someone's home,
but they had to secure the use of a church annex building.
They started with the use of the Houston Road Church of God
social hall building. This was the church the majority of the
Stokes' attended. As the years progressed, various churches
in the Warner Robins area were utilized.

Quinelle was proud to be a part of this family; such a loving, caring, and God-fearing family. They had always made
her feel welcome from the beginning. Pete's family had become her family. She is grateful to see her children and their
cousins be a part of such a close-knit family.

Granddaddy, Pete's Dad, is sorely missed at these gatherings. It's just not the same without his presence. Taking his
time, he would open his gifts with his pocket knife...very slowly.
The kids would surround him to see what he had received,
and would get agitated at his lack of speed to get the gift

opened. He would just laugh that almost inaudible laugh of his, knowing he was vexing the children.

The next Christmas celebration for the Pete Stokes family was Christmas Eve with the children and grandchildren. They would always meet at Pete and Quinelle's house. Quinelle had done all of the shopping, of course, and was looking forward to this time spent with her family. There were three stepchildren now. Lonnie's youngest, Kayle, came to live with them. He had been living with his Mother in Texas, but was now here permanently. Now, she had eight grandchildren to shop for.

The shopping doesn't usually wear her out like it has this year. She is feeling fatigued too much, she thinks to herself. She is bloated much of the time, and looks like she is about three months pregnant. Even Pete kidded her about this in front of the children during their Christmas Eve get-together. She just laughs right along with them, but knows that something is not right.

Her children ask her repeatedly if she is all right. They can tell by her lack of enthusiasm that she does not feel well. She is making every effort to try to conceal her discomfort.

The gifts are unwrapped, the grandchildren are playing with their toys, the girls are cleaning up the kitchen while she remains seated by the fireplace. She is very tired and wants to go to bed.

The family comes in to wish her Merry Christmas and say their good-byes. Many memories were made tonight. She just wishes she could have enjoyed the evening more.

She determines in her mind that she can and will wait until January to get a doctor's appointment. Lord, help me get through the rest of this month, she prays as she climbs the stairs to the bedroom.

Chapter 49

The birthday party was over. The children and grandkids had come over to the house to celebrate Quinelle's birthday – her 49th. She never let on to her family just how badly she was feeling. Only Pete knew of her doctor's appointment the following day.

Before the end of the next day, Quinelle had been admitted into the hospital. The first plan of action was to drain off the fluid that had built up in her stomach. There were blood tests to be done and various other tests performed. The following day surgery was scheduled to determine the advancement of the cancer. While in surgery, they performed an hysterectomy in the event the cancer had spread to her female organs.

The children came to visit after the surgery had been performed. They were informed by Pete that the doctors had issued a prognosis of no more than six months to live. The cancer was in such an aggressive state that there was nothing more the doctors could do for her.

Arriving home from the hospital a few days later, she was inundated with visits from friends and family. She really did appreciate the care and concern everyone expressed, but was not up to the task. She just wanted to be left alone.

Pete very rarely left her side. He had decided to halt any more construction projects that were in the works. His priority was to take care of his wife. She needed his encouragement and support more than anything. They prayed many times daily for her strength and her healing. They were not going to give up on God. This was indeed a major setback in their plans, but knew God could intervene if that was His will to do so. They prayed that he would choose to intervene.

Quinelle was never one to complain about her circumstances nor question God, but this particular day she was in anguish about her situation. Why, God, is this happening to me? I'm too young to die. Pete and I have plans to travel. What about my grandchildren that have yet to be born? I'll never get to know them. She began to sob hysterically.

Pete overheard the sobs coming from the upstairs bedroom. He ran hurriedly up the stairs.

"What is wrong?" Pete asked as he sat on the edge of the bed and held her.

"I'm just emotional right now, Pete. I'll be okay."

"Talk to me, sweetheart," Pete requested. "Maybe there is something I can do to help if I know what is bothering you."

"I just don't want to die. I'm too young. I don't want to leave you."

Pete held her for a few moments, then proceeded to kneel down beside the bed. He prayed for her state of mind asking God to intercede, and to heal her body of this cancer.

When he ended his prayer, he said, "Quinelle, this is one thing I can do for you, and that is to pray for you. We will read Scripture together every day to reinforce our faith and trust in Jesus. Now, let me help you get dressed."

"Thanks, Pete. But first, I want you to look in my top dresser drawer. There's a poem I would like for you to read. This is from me to you.

Pete opened up the drawer and found a slip of paper with these typewritten words:

I love you in a thousand ways
Beneath a thousand skies
As I have known you all these years
And gazed into your eyes
You are so wonderful to me
In every loving way
Forever in my thoughts and dreams
And every time I pray
I wish that could pay you back
In just the smallest measure
For all that you have given me
To hold and always treasure
But this much I can promise you
I am your very own
And all the happiness I have
Depends on you alone
I love you and I promise you
Whatever I may be
That no one else in all the world
Will mean so much to me.

Chapter 50

Quinelle has become too weak to maneuver up and down the stairs any longer to their bedroom and bathroom. A hospital bed has been added to the living room décor placed strategically in front of *the picture window*. She had made this request so she would be able to see the flowers and dogwoods in bloom.

"Remember when we planted together these azaleas and dogwoods?" Pete asked Quinelle as they both stood near the hospital bed, admiring the beauty of a number of the azaleas that were already blooming.

"Oh, yes. Hard to believe that was about ten years ago. We did a good job, didn't we?"

"We wanted to be farmers again; we planted a large garden for a few years – until we grew tired of all the work." With that, they both laughed.

Quinelle replied, "I sure did enjoy those years of growing our own peanuts. You know me – how much I enjoy boiled peanuts. I'd almost make myself sick from eating so many."

Becoming pensive Quinelle turns to sit on the hospital bed, "I don't like having to sleep down here without you by my side, but this is better than being in the hospital."

Pete sits beside her, taking her hands in his, "I don't relish the idea of our sleeping apart. But, this way you can probably get more sleep; my snoring keeps you awake sometimes, I know.

"You do snore loudly at times. I'll probably be able to hear you down here."

Quinelle chuckled. It felt good to laugh.

April 1982

It's here – the first day of April – the beginning of my fourth month of hibernation in this house.

The picture window was framing the springtime in a majestic manner. The tall pines gently swaying in the breeze were very stately. They looked as if they were reaching up into the heavens and praising our Lord and Saviour.

Oh, dear, there are so many family members with birthdays this month, and I don't have the stamina to shop for cards and gifts. I guess I will have to get Pete to do it for me this year.

As if on cue, Pete entered the room with some toast and watermelon juice. "Breakfast is served, my dear," placing the plate on the tray next to her bed.

"Pete, I have a favor to ask you. There are several birthdays coming up this month. Some I just want to send cards and others we need to get gifts for."

"Okay," Pete hesitantly replied. He was not one to shop for cards and gifts. Quinelle always took care of that chore! "Whose birthdays are coming up?"

"Your Momma's for one. Then there's Willene, Gwen, Danna, and Neilie. Just get cards for your Momma and Willene, but we do need gifts for the others."

Quinelle could see the blank look on Pete's face. "I tell you what, would you rather I ask Connie to handle this for us?"

"Would you, please? She will better at this than I will."

"Your Momma's and Willene's are in just two days. Call Connie right away. Maybe she can take care of these two cards at the least today."

"I'll do that right now."

Pete left me for a time. I try my best to get my toast down, but haven't much of an appetite lately. I wonder how much weight I have lost, or maybe I actually don't want to know.

Sunday, Mother's Day, May 1982

"It's a gorgeous day, sweetheart, "Pete exclaimed as he drew back the curtains. "Happy Mother's Day."

"Thanks. I guess the children will be coming by after church. They usually do, anyway, on Sundays."

"Yes, the plans are for two o'clock, to celebrate Mother's Day with you."

"I hope they don't bring gifts. I don't need anything, and won't need anything. I'm not sure I'm up to this today. I don't want the grandchildren to see me like this. Please tell them not to bring the kids in here."

Pete could see the angst on her face. He knew this was ripping her apart not to see the grandchildren.

"I'll tell the children when they get here," Pete told her as he leaned over and kissed her forehead.

Quinelle closed her eyes. The pain was more intense the past few days. The medication and shots of morphine kept her sedated the majority of the time now.

She awoke to the sound of voices. The children came bearing cards and gifts. Pete helped her to sit up; then each one hugged her neck, and wished her a happy Mother's day.

They each handed her a card and a gift. Pete opened the gifts for her.

"Why did you waste your money on these gifts?" Quinelle said in a tone of voice so unlike herself.

This question caught everyone off guard. No one knew what to say for a moment.

"Because you're our Mother and we have to buy you something," Chris retorted with the typical humor that he was notorious for. He was hoping to get a laugh out of her.

Quinelle looked around at her children. These were her blessings from above. She would miss them so! This thought caused her much distress; so much so that Pete asked the children to leave.

They all gathered around her bed and told her that they loved her and would be praying for her.

After they all departed, she turned her head toward the picture window and cried.

Her heart was breaking. Lord, help me!

May 17, 1982

I hear subtle voices in the background. I open my eyes and see the curtains are drawn over *the picture window*. It must be dark outside. I struggle to move to see who is in the room.

Pete is immediately at my side. He must be staying in here with me because he's always right here when I wake.

I hear moaning. Is that me? I try to speak, but so difficult to get the words out.

Pete tries to get me to drink something. I haven't the energy to swallow.

I can see Chris, Gwen, Kevin, and Connie standing all around my bed. They are praying for God to take the pain away. They are still expecting God to heal me. Kevin is praying in the Spirit. His voice rises up and down.

I think the battle is over for me. I am too tired to fight anymore.

I reach for Chris' hand and try to tell him that I need to speak with him. He understands and leans his ear to my lips. I ask him, "Do I always have to do what everybody tells me to do?"

Chris looked puzzled. "What did you say?" as he bent down even closer.

"Do I always have to do what everybody tells me to do?"

"I don't know what you are struggling with, but you have

always make good decisions. So, whatever you think you need to do, it will be the right thing."

I release his hand out of sheer exhaustion. Connie and Gwen come closer. They are laying their hands on top of my hands.

Next time I opened my eyes, they had left my bedside. Instead, there was my sweetheart standing over me, caressing my hair. He was holding my hand. I squeeze his hand with what little strength I have left. He got down on his knees beside the bed, and looked me in the eyes.

"What is it, Quinelle?"

"I need for you to let me go," I told him as our eyes locked together.

I could see the pain in his eyes – the pain of letting me go was as much for him to bear as was my physical pain to me.

I could feel his hand stiffen. It took him a few moments before he spoke. With reluctance in his voice, he whispered to me ever so gently, "Okay, sweetheart, I will let you go."

And he did.

Epilogue

Quinelle died in the early morning hours of May 18, 1982. She was facing the picture window. God had called her home. She was healed.

The library Quinelle initiated at the Haynesville Assembly of God church was named in her memory, and still exists today.

> Quinelle and Pete's <u>children</u>, grandchildren and great grandchildren are as listed:
> <u>Connie's</u> children: Neilie and Heather
> <u>Chris's</u> children: Shane, Luke, Danna
> <u>Gwen's</u> children: Joshua and Lindsey (born after Quinelle's death)
> <u>Great Grandchildren</u>
> Neilie's children: Jacob, Jon, and Ashlynn
> Heather's children: Dalton and Trey
> Shane's children: Casidey, Sierra, and Kristen
> Luke was killed in an automobile accident in 2000. He had married but had no children.
> Danna's children: Cheyan

Pete remarried and has been married now to Brenda Rowland for almost thirty years. They reside in Perry, Georgia.

Afterword

I felt compelled to write my Mother's story. My only experience in writing were scripts for television and radio commercials. I gradually began gathering information via my Mothers papers from high school, and interviewing family members. The summer of 2013, I felt a real urgency to get this into book form. I began immediately to give more of my time to researching family history, and more interviews were performed.

My Mother, Quinelle Yeomans Stokes, was not only my Mother, but my source of inspiration. She still is!

About the Author

The author resides in Perry, Georgia with her husband, Tommy, when not at their mountain cabin located in Otto, North Carolina. The majority of *The Picture Window* was written while relaxing in the cabin appropriately named "Haven on Earth".